Reviews for *Twisted Reveries*

"The author has a vivid imagination, but there's always some underlying structure, a reason, a tie-in between the macabre events that are happening and the history of the person involved in the events. It's not as though everything happens willy-nilly. There are reasons at work. That sense of structure, so essential, she creates successfully." John W.

"Horrifically compelling stories full of fascinating concepts that draw you in, keeping you transfixed to the surprising end." Andrea S.

"A beautiful blend of suspense, horror, and humor, like a blend of Dean Koontz and Edgar Allen Poe." Tobias K.

"I'm not particularly drawn to tales of the macabre, so I was particularly DELIGHTED to have found this experience so utterly enjoyable. The author is so effective in creating a reader who becomes engaged and focused and excited to read on. To me, that is the epitome of a good writer." Kathy W.

"I loved the book. I appreciated a female voice in horror and it reflected in the characters. The stories included had a good balance of mystery and horror that kept me on the edge of my seat many times." Kelly F.

Meg Hafdahl

Twisted Reveries
13 Tales of the Macabre

by

Meg Hafdahl

R.I.P
(Read in Peace)

Inklings
Publishing
www.inklingspublishing.com

First U.S. Edition

Edited by Fern Brady

Editorial Services, Johnnie Bernhard 808-227-0682

Cover Art by Verstandt

ISBN: 978-0-9910211-7-8 by Inklings Publishing
http://inklingspublishing.com

DEDICATION

To Mom: you taught me to love reading.

To Dad: you taught me to love writing.

CONTENTS

ACKNOWLEDGMENTS

I would like to thank Fern Brady for her wisdom, insight and patience. Without Fern this book would still be banging about in my head, unfinished and horribly unpolished.

I couldn't have done this without Luke. Thank you for always telling the truth, even when you were scared to...

Fox and Dexter, my two precious boys, I will forever be trying to be a better person for you, working to somehow be worthy of being your mother.

Kelly, thank you for dreaming big. Jen, thanks for putting up with me longer than anyone. To all my friends and family, your support and love fuels me.

I would like to acknowledge CCFA.org. I have Crohn's Disease, as does the main character in *Guts*. I encourage you to check out the website and, if you're inspired, volunteer or donate, so we can find a cure.

Lastly, I would like to tip my proverbial hat to all the women authors who came before me. The women who were drawn to the darker side; the women who wrote of real, flawed females. And most of all, to the women who were not afraid.

Meg Hafdahl

Moira Kettlesburg

Moira Kettlesburg, sixty years old and head librarian of the Otter Tail County Branch Library in Willoughby, Minnesota, headed down Main Street with her sack lunch tucked under her armpit. The kids had taken to calling her a media specialist. That's what they called Roma Fellows at the school, but, just like most new things, Moira rejected this title vehemently.

She was a librarian, dammit.

She knew books. She used the Dewey Decimal System. She taught the children to search with their eyes and their brains. They were encouraged to ask Moira for help, rather than punch titles into a screen. Moira believed all children needed to live through that awkward, precarious moment when they had to disrupt the silence of the library and approach the librarian. It built character.

Today turned out to be a terribly windy day, Moira's carefully curled red coif unfurled into a ghastly sight. She unlocked the glass front door, still holding her lunch under one arm, and pushed her way inside. Sometimes she wished she could just move in already, build an apartment in the library basement, and never leave. Then she wouldn't have to walk downhill from her decaying house on Oak Lane. Then she wouldn't have to share a kitchen with her eternally pinched older sister. Then she could live like a true nun, alone and silent, down in her cloisters. But instead of God, it was books she would worship.

An extended trip to the bathroom fixed her hair. Soon Moira, dressed in her usual dark slacks and white blouse, settled in to her morning routine. The same one she had begun thirty years ago when she was hired to start a library in her hometown. She brewed coffee in her trusty pot, a bit rusted, but more reliable than that strange Keurig abomination she had received from the book club girls. They had all pitched in and bought it for her for Christmas. She forced a smile and pretended to read the features on the box, all the while wondering what on earth was wrong with her coffee maker.

It was Tuesday. So the moms would be coming with the children, the very young ones with snot bubbling from their nostrils and soft shoes. It was toddler story time every Tuesday, and in the summer it was still quite popular. Moira placed a copy of *Don't Let the Pigeon Drive the Bus!* on her story time chair, along with a few hand puppets, as old and worn as the coffee maker, that aided in the morning songs.

Moira knew she would be flying solo today. Her summer helper, a teen girl with an unremarkable name and an even less memorable face, went on a family trip to somewhere with roller coasters. She would not return for two weeks. This meant Moira had to do all the menial tasks, like digging out the returns from the bin and re-shelving. But of course she loved it all, even handling the sticky kid's books and helping the tourists find their James Patterson novels, or perhaps Nicholas Sparks, just something fluffy to leave on a beach towel as they swam in one of Minnesota's 10,000 lakes.

Early morning was Moira's favorite part of the day. She had a solid hour before she had to open the library, to share it. So now she got her mug of black coffee and placed it in her usual spot, the reading area between non-fiction and the children's section, where the large picture window, in need of a cleaning Moira noted, over looked the Main Street of Willoughby. She then retrieved the plastic return bin on wheels from its spot under the metal return slot fused into the side of the brick building. Moira pulled it with two hands, across the thin carpet and next to her waiting coffee and a book trolley she used to organize by Dewey.

She sat in a hard backed chair, one normally reserved for teenagers working on a school report, and got to work, pulling out books and placing them on the trolley according to their number. Moira had read most of the novels. Each time she placed her fingers on one a memory would come to her of the world she had lived in for a few, fleeting hours. She had lived thousands, millions, of lives in her books.

Yet, as she watched the people of Willoughby rally for another Tuesday, she couldn't help but think she had forgotten to live her own life. She forgot to get married, she was reminded of that every day her mother had been alive. Evangeline Kettlesburg had even mentioned it to Moira while on her literal death bed, in her passive aggressive manner of course, the Minnesota non-confrontational way her mother always employed.

Moira forgot to have children, too, she was reminded of that every time her eyes skimmed the bright colors of the children's section.

Her sister, Glenda, went to college and got married and then divorced, and then married again. She had a daughter and now two grandsons. Then her second husband, an asshole from the start, dropped dead from a bad heart.

Now both Moira and Glenda were living in Evangeline's old house, alone yet together, their end the same. So maybe all that in-between stuff wasn't necessary after all.

Moira tried to make herself believe this.

She placed each book, not really looking, not really needing to. She watched the farmers trickle out of the café into the irresistibly beautiful summer morning. The wind pushed at their backs and pulled at their caps, but it was still a nearly perfect day. She watched Doug Deacon, the funeral director, smoke one of those electronic cigarettes, as he leaned against the side of his business. She watched two girls, twelve or thirteen perhaps, emerge from the small grocery store. One swung a plastic bag, filled with candy no doubt, while the other pushed her purple bike along the sidewalk.

There was something about the young girls that made her remember. A memory, visceral and unexpected, stung Moira's heart. It was of Henry, of his face.

She was used to seeing him in her dreams. He was there nearly every night, his usually happy, young, handsome self. And she would reach out to him and he wouldn't come. Couldn't come.

Now, she let the paperback, *Rebecca* by Daphne DuMaurier, slide back into the bin and closed her eyes, embracing her painful memory. She could suddenly remember the curl of his yellow hair and the few, subtle pockmarks on his chin; from a bad bout of chicken pox he had told her.

She remembered his bathing trunks that last day, blue and white checks, and how the lining kept poking out the top as they kissed in the sand.

Moira lost his face. He faded away from her, as he did in her dreams. She finally opened her eyes and took a long, comforting sip of coffee.

"Henry," she whispered to the empty library. Her lips trembled on his name.

And then, for some reason she could never afterward define, in that moment, on that summer Tuesday, forty years later, Moira was sure he hadn't left her on purpose.

Henry died that night. She had spent the last four decades telling herself he had dumped her, left her, given her up. That she deserved it somehow; that she was better off anyways. But now, now, she was finally sure. In this moment, gazing out onto Main Street, surrounded by her shelves of books, she could finally accept it.

He was dead.

Dead.

Moira felt an intense mix of relief and dread. Now that she was sixty, now that she was in the last few scrapes of life, there was an answer to the single question that pulled at her; how could he? How could he leave her with just a hastily scrawled note? They were in love; they were soulmates; she had believed this, before the world dragged her down. Before Henry tore her apart with his absence. But she knew now, somehow now, he had never left her. That he died in Willoughby. That he was somewhere, whatever place it was that dead people go. And when he went, when he arrived there, he was probably still in his blue and white checked swimming trunks.

And so Moira Kettlesburg did something she had never done in her nearly thirty years of service for Otter Tail County. She wrote a note of her own, on a piece of printer paper, declaring the library closed for the day. She taped it to the front door, vaguely sorry for the moms and the toddlers and the tourists in need of a beach read. But she was only slightly regretful, because she felt there had been a death, a very sudden death, which she had never mourned, not properly.

She bounded up Main, oddly quiet now, back up the hill toward Oak. Her legs burned with effort, she was more of a reader than an outdoors woman after all, but the fresh wind in her lungs and the glimmer of sun made her feel triumphant. She felt she had unlocked some secret buried in her brain. Moira knew all along he was dead, from the moment, all those years ago, she opened the screen door, and saw the flapping yellow paper with dark letters bleeding through.

Moira,

On to somewhere new. Thanks for the memories.

H

Her twenty-year-old-self read the words over and over. She crumpled the paper, smoothed it out, and crumpled it again. She was sure she would die from the heartbreak. Moira could still remember the physical pain. How her heart actually hurt, how it thudded dully in her young chest.

Her mother said she knew it was going to happen, a blond boy was going to break her. She was always going after the blond boys, the funny ones with bright blue eyes.

"Glen? Glenda!" Moira swung through that same screen door into their sprawling family home. Sepia pictures of their parents dotted the walls. An old display hutch held their father's wood carvings of birds and foxes.

Moira followed the smell of bacon into the kitchen, last decorated in the Sixties with the latest Formica counters and wood paneled cabinets. Her older sister, barefoot, hovered by the stove, looking as though she had been caught doing something devious. She was still in her nightgown and terry cloth robe.

"What the hell? Did you forget your lunch?" Glenda, only sixty-four but wrinkled and grey beyond her years, pushed her glasses up her narrow nose to get a better look at Moira.

Moira shook her head. "I need you to get your laptop, bring it down."

Glenda's eyes squinted underneath the thick lenses. "What are you doing here Moira?"

"Oh just get it already, I'll watch your bacon." She stepped forward and took the pan handle in her fingers. "I'll flip 'em."

Glenda shrugged and began her ascent up the back stairs. It would take her several minutes to find the thing and then lug it down to the kitchen. Her annoyance with her librarian sister palpable.

As Moira stared at the crackling meat, she willed herself to see Henry again. She wanted to see his face once more, on command, not just the vague outline of handsomeness she normally resorted to, but his real face, the one she studied forty summers ago. It did not come.

Glenda huffed down the steps, her knees audibly cracking with each stair. "This better be good," she croaked. The laptop, a gift from her daughter, was dramatically plopped onto the kitchen table.

Moira removed the bacon from the pan and placed the strips on a paper plate lined with a napkin. She handed the breakfast to her sister.

"I need you to look someone up." She put on her own glasses, tucked in her pants pocket for reading, in order to see the monitor. Glenda obliged, sitting down and then clicking into Google with such natural ease it made Moira cringe.

"Type in Henry Arnold Jacobbson, two Bs."

"Oh you can't be serious!" Glenda screeched. "Moira!"

Moira stood behind her sister. "Yes I'm serious, Glen, someone must be missing him."

Glenda turned. Her eyes were now comically large and circular behind her glasses. "Moira, get over it! Do you really care this much?"

Yes, yes she cared. She had never stopped. All those people that told her time would heal her wounds were wrong. Moira felt as if it had all happened yesterday, leaving her raw and unhinged. She used books as an escape, a time gap, a buffer between herself and reality. And perhaps that was it, perhaps she had read nearly all the books in the Willoughby branch and she was left with no other alternative than to face the truth.

"Type in his name." She swallowed down all the other words that wanted to come screaming out at her sister. She did need Glenda's tech savvy after all.

Glenda punched in the name, her mouth a straight line of disapproval. There were baby announcements for Henry Jacob so and so, and political articles by someone named Henry Arnold. At the bottom of the first search page there was a link to a Facebook page, find my brother: Henry Arnold Jacobbson.

"Oh my God," Moira sucked in a nauseous breath. "Click on it, click!"

She saw his picture first, on the left hand side of the page. She had never seen a picture of him before. He was a bit younger, and his hair was a bit shaggier, but it was him; it was her Henry.

> My name is DeAnne and my big brother, Henry, has been missing since 1975. He was twenty-two years old. He left our home in Duluth, MN, to make his way across the state on a solo nature trip and never returned. If you know anything, or if you just want to share a memory of Henry, please post on this page.
> Thanks!

Moira sank into the chair next to Glenda. Realization burned through her. "How long has this page been online?"

"Um, looks like 2009. There are some posts, just looks like his high school friends reminiscing." Glenda scrolled down with the mouse.

Six years. For six years she could have had comfort. She could have known. He was dead; he really was dead. She chided herself for not knowing before that moment. If only she knew how to use a damn computer.

~

Moira fell in love with Henry when he called himself a poet. Specifically a nature poet, a romantic, who wrote odes to pinecones, instead of urns, he joked. He was too shy to share his journal, a tattered thing resting under his hands at the City Café, where she had worked that summer. She had served him his pie and a Coke, and nearly tripped over her own feet.

Sometimes she wondered when he'd fallen in love with her. She wished they had married and grown old together, so she could ask him a silly question like that.

They had three weeks together. And sometimes this was enough for her. Sometimes she could remember those weeks with a fondness, a happiness. But more often she wished they had never happened, because her life went perpetually downhill after that summer.

~

Now, feeling a bit like Miss Marple, she used old fashioned methods to find a phone number for DeAnne, still living in Duluth. Glenda made sure to tell her how silly she was being, that nothing had changed, that he had left a break up note for her. But Moira was seized with a motivation she had never known before. Henry was dead and she had to know why. And she had to know how it had happened; she just couldn't believe it was an accident, that didn't ring true.

"Hello?" A woman's gravelly voice answered.

"Hello, yes, is this DeAnne Jacobbson?" Moira twirled the olive colored phone cord around her wrist.

The woman waited a beat. "Well it's not Jacobbson anymore…"

"Oh, of course. Well, I'm calling about Henry." Just saying his name once more, acknowledging his existence made Moira's skin flush.

DeAnne didn't respond for a full five seconds. Finally, she cleared her throat. "Henry, my brother?"

"I saw your Facebook page. I…I got a hold of your number. My name is Moira." Moira could hear the nervousness in her own voice. She attempted her approachable librarian lilt, but it came out stuttering.

"Okay," DeAnne sounded suspicious. "So, did you know my brother?"

"Yes, we…yes, I knew him that summer of 1975. We fell in love. He was coming through my town, Willoughby, we're out near Fergus Falls. Anyway, we met and he stayed and we were going to go away together. And then one morning there was a strange note on my door, saying he left without me. But, but I really don't think, no, no, I know he wouldn't have left me. I know that now. I think he disappeared from here, from Willoughby."

There was silence on the other side of the line. Moira could almost visualize her lover's little sister, in her fifties now, considering her words.

"What day was it? I mean, the date?" DeAnne asked.

"July 6, 1975." Moira knew exactly. She stood in her kitchen, the same kitchen, and remembered. She remembered crying at the table, and Glenda, home from college, handing her tissues.

"Moira, I believe you." DeAnne breathed into the receiver. "My parents last got a letter from him on July 1st. He said he'd met a girl. He said he was going to marry you."

The tears came then, unexpected but welcomed. Moira couldn't remember the last time she had cried for herself, for Henry. She only cried for books now, the really sad and good ones.

~

Glenda was waiting for her on the porch. She had poured two glasses of sweet tea before sitting in their grandfather's frayed rattan rocking chair. The summer morning was becoming a steamy afternoon.

"Who's watching the library?" Glenda ran a skinny finger around the rim of her sweating glass of tea.

Moira pressed a tissue under her soggy eyes to collect the tears. She fell into a cushioned bench next to Glenda's rocker. "No one."

A ghost of something, straining and worrisome, crossed Glenda's features. She puckered her lips, twisting them from side to side as she considered her little sister.

"DeAnne says he mentioned me in a letter," Moira took a gulp from her glass. "But that makes me think, then why didn't the police come down here? They had a postmark from his last known whereabouts."

"Whereabouts?" Glenda huffed. "Moira, what on Earth? Why now?"

"Do you think it's because of that girl? They didn't care about some guy disappearing because of that twelve year old? The one that went missing before him, a week or so before. Remember? The police were so wrapped up in her case, God, for years they were," Moira buzzed with all the history, all the facts.

Glenda watched.

The taste of sweet tea on Moira's tongue struck another memory; Henry on the porch, when there was a swing, of a glass of cold tea pressed between her bare thighs. She could remember his faintly calloused hands, roaming everywhere.

Why now? She wondered.

"I feel that I have been in a fog." Moira straightened up out of her slump. "I feel today, just today, I have figured it out."

Glenda leaned forward. Her knobby, arthritic hands clutched at her knees. "Figured what out?"

Moira raised her chin. She savored the sweetness in her mouth, the smell of basil from their garden, the warm breeze sweeping onto the porch.

"Henry died on the night of July 5th. After a summer day, one just like this. And someone wrote that note, someone else."

Before her big sister could hiss in protest, Moira bounded down the steps and onto the sidewalk. She wanted to look back, she wanted to see Glenda's enormous eyes and disappointed frown. It would be fun to see her sputter. Yet she stopped herself. There was no more looking back, only looking ahead. She was going into the woods. She was going to find Henry.

~

For the first time in four decades Moira Kettlesburg walked the narrow trail to Cross Lake. The sun filtered through the thick trees and the brambles, but she was mostly shaded. The last time, she could remember now in vivid detail, she was walking back alone in her swimsuit. It was a yellow bikini, the bottoms sticky with Henry, and she was swinging her tote bag while singing a rather loud and shaky version of "Lady Marmalade." It was the last time she was happy.

Now she moved quickly on the trail. She was not young anymore. She was not relishing nature, or an afternoon of delicious lovemaking. Instead she was channeling all those books, all those characters she had lived with her entire adult life. She thought of Miss Marple, whom would surely join her on this journey, and of Sherlock and Watson. They probably wouldn't have waited forty years to solve a crime.

Oops. I suppose I should have done this sooner. Moira thought. But no, no I wasn't ready. I hadn't been ready until now, until today.

Her shoes, the comfy, squishy sort she had transitioned to from her signature mules after a nasty winter fall, were sinking into a bit of mud. She knew she was close. Sweat trickled down her back.

Cross Lake was the same.

There was a pack of boisterous teenagers on the far end, girls screeching in delight as the boys dragged them in the water.

It was nice to see nothing had really changed.

There were a few families, organized moms, children slathered in sunscreen, exhausted dads. But Moira looked past them all. Her eyes were glued to the log cabin on the edge of the water.

It was still there, the place he rented. She had never bothered to come back, to check it. She just buried herself. She just curled up in a fantasy world. Moira hated herself at that moment. She hated how she had been a coward and let herself fall into the imagined worlds her books provided. It wasn't her beloved books' fault; it was her own fear that had controlled her.

"Ms. Kettlesburg!" A voice from the mix of people on the beach. Moira continued, pressing through the sand. Her feet ached and her cheeks felt like they were on fire in the open sun.

"Moira!"

The cabin beckoned to her from across the lake. It looked the same.

The same.

"Moira? Are you okay?" A woman touched her shoulder. Moira swung around, irritated.

The woman, a mom from story time, a daughter of an old friend, removed her sunglasses and watched Moira. "We missed you this morning." A small child buzzed around her knees. "Are you okay? You must be melting in those clothes."

Moira looked down at her work attire, dappled with sweat. Her favorite necklace, an owl on a gold chain clattered against her breasts.

"Yes, I suppose so." She ran a hand through her hair. "I have to go to that cabin over there." She pointed. "Do you know much about it?"

The mom raised an eyebrow. "No, I think it's empty. Just animals live in it now. We don't let the kids over there." She stared at Moira, the same ghost of concern crossed her young face that had passed over Glenda's.

"Oh." Moira turned, determined to finish her trek around the lake. She knew the woman, whatever her name was, it had slipped from her as she stood watching her just as her sister had. Her look a combination of pity and worry Moira assumed. But what they all didn't know was that Moira Kettlesburg, head librarian, was finally awake.

The cabin was under a thick layer of dirt and vegetation. But it was still the same. There was the small porch, now covered in dead, brittle leaves and animal poop. There was the small, circular window at the top where you could look out from the loft. She trailed a hand over the rough logs, remembering.

Henry rented the place from Frank Johns. He liked how it was both right on the beach and nestled in the woods. He was inspired to write. That's why she had left him that day. He wanted to write his poetry. Moira believed there was no nobler motivation in all the world. So she had dressed in her yellow bikini and kissed his cheek.

"I'm going to write one about you." He was in his swim trunks, his notebook already in hand. "Moira, Goddess of the Forest," Henry smiled. He had pointy incisors, which made his smile all the more adorable and unique. "Moira in the bright, teeny bikini, a vision of immortal beauty, sashaying about in the lush landscape of a Minnesota summer…"

"Oh alright!" Moira had the distinct impression he was making fun of her. She snuggled into his warm, tanned body. He had a tiny patch of fuzzy, blonde hair on his chest. She buried her nose in it and breathed in his scent.

"I'll pick you up in the morning, we'll get pancakes." He took her face in his large hands and kissed her firmly. "I love you."

"I love you, too." Moira said for the last time in her life.

~

Now, she stood in the same cabin, in the same room. It was oddly cold. Henry's bed was gone, as well as the roll top desk he used for writing. There was an overturned bucket, perhaps used by a squatter for a makeshift chair. The smell of urine filled the room in a gagging cloud.

Moira wanted to be logical. She thought of Frank Johns, long dead. She could have asked him questions, and the local police, and the Duluth police. All retired now, or dead, or maybe in nursing homes with tubes up their noses. Forty years was a long time. For forty years there had been summers and winters and life, yet no Henry.

What did she expect to find here? Another note? An arrow, pointed to the ground? And then she would dig with her bare hands until she found a skeleton, one holding a book of poems and wearing blue and white checked swimming trunks?

Blue and white swimming trunks. Blue and white checks. Blue and white.

She was forgetting something. There was something locked inside, buried underneath the books and the routine and her excuse of a life. Something she wasn't ready for. Something it took forty years to process.

Blue and white checks. Blue and white checks on fire.

Moira sunk to the filthy floor. She wasn't Miss Marple and she was no Sherlock. She wanted only to help Henry, to set him free, to set herself free.

A creak.

Perhaps it was Henry. Dripping wet from a swim, his blonde hair sticking up. Maybe he was coming back, a bit late, and he was here to take her hand and bring her to the place, the place he had been, where dead people go.

Moira kneeled on the floor, hoping, hoping.

Another creak and then a shuffle.

"Moira?" A timid voice.

"Glenda?" Moira pressed her eyes closed. She couldn't let the memories slip now, she couldn't lose his face.

"Yes." Glenda stood behind her.

There was a sudden influx of unwelcome memories. A darkness fell upon Moira. She struggled to organize her mind.

"Why did you kill Henry?" The words came out before she could really think them. Before they could form in her mind. She remained staring forward, afraid to look behind her.

She could hear Glenda give a shaky sigh, and then slump to the floor on her knees too. The movement must have hurt her sister's arthritic joints.

"You must know why." Glenda's voice, although weak and tinny, filled the abandoned cabin.

Moira curled her body forward. She felt physical pain in her belly; a hot searing rage mixed with a sick uncertainty.

The wind picked up outside, shuffling dead leaves on the porch and rattling the thin windowpanes.

"I keep thinking about those blue and white checked trunks, the ones he wore that last day…" Moira looked down at the dirty wood floor. "Why? Why do you think?"

Glenda dragged herself closer to her sister. Moira could feel Glenda behind her, too close. "He was wearing lime green trunks, Moira, I'm sure."

What a silly thing. What a trivial thing. Yet it mattered somehow.

"No." Moira shook her head. She spread both hands on the floor and dug her nails into the soft wood. "No."

Glenda reached out her thin hand. She stopped herself from resting it on Moira's shoulder. Instead she pushed a puff of grey hair away from her glasses. "You're confusing the fire, the blue and white checks you told me about, with what he was wearing. That night, the last night, he had lime green trunks. I know because he was chasing me. And all I could see, God, all I could see were those green swimming trunks, through the trees."

Moira finally twisted around to face Glenda. "I don't…you're not making any sense."

They locked eyes. It had been a long while, years probably, since Moira had really looked at her sister, really noticed her. It was terrifying to see her big sister beaten by life.

"Moira, you know. You know what he did."

"No."

"He was a bad man."

"No. No. Not Henry."

"You told me about the fire. The one he started here, the one you walked in on, you surprised him." A tear escaped the suction of Glenda's thick glasses and dripped down her nightdress.

"No, I…I just said it was odd." Moira froze.

Blue and white checks on fire.

Not swimming trunks, no, something else.

Something with lace trim and pearl buttons.

The memory floated up, like a balloon, untethered and free. Moira had come to surprise him, at dawn. She couldn't sleep. She loved him too much to ever sleep. He was poking at a fire. She thought he would be curled in bed. But instead Henry was in jeans and no shirt, prodding the fire in a makeshift pit with a large stick. His eyes had lost their usual joviality. She had been scared of his face. He had looked different, wrong.

Blue and white checks.

"That girl." The name tumbled from her, again before she could truly process it. "Tara. The missing one."

Glenda shut her eyes. Her sister nodded up and down, the weight of it all clearly leaving her body. She had carried it all for too long. Long enough to make her sour, pinched and tired of life.

"That was Tara's dress you saw in the fire, and you knew it, you knew but you couldn't..."

"Believe it?" Moira swallowed down a lump of tears. "Oh shit Glenda." She crawled toward her sister and wrapped two trembling arms around her.

They held each other for the first time as grownups.

"Henry KILLED that little girl..." Moira sobbed into Glenda's chest. "And he tried to kill you, didn't he? Didn't he?"

Glenda didn't speak. She softly ran her palms across Moira's hair. It reminded Moira of their mother's reassuring pats.

Moira felt she could sink into the floor, become a human puddle and never get up. Tara, twelve years old and in the place where dead people go, had seen Henry for what he really was.

She wondered why. She wondered if there were other girls, across the state, a trail of them from Duluth to Willoughby, dead by Henry's hands.

Why did he love Moira? Why did he not kill her? What was the difference?

"Did you bury him under the ground?" Moira sniffed.

Glenda didn't answer.

There were so many questions, a million. How did she do it? A gun, a knife, a rock? Did she have to do it? What if Moira hadn't told her sister about the blue and white checks in the fire? God, what if she had kept her mouth shut?

But Glenda saved her. Because Moira would have had been foolish enough to marry him.

And Glenda preserved Henry's memory, however erroneous, to create happiness for her little sister. Moira had known. Really, she had.

Moira recognized the handwriting on the note taped to the screen door. She had noticed Glenda's dirty fingernails and her pale, scared eyes the next morning. She had known, later, whose blue and white checked sundress was burning that morning.

Yet it was easier to put Henry on a pedestal all these years, and leave her sister to do the remembering. How strange to realize she was not the heroine of her own story.

Moira Kettlesburg, head librarian, stopped crying.

She rose, suddenly aware of her aged muscles, and inhaled the stale air. She brushed dirt off her black pants and scraped at the mud on her shoes. Her big sister, her protector, remained on the cabin floor, old and quiet.

Moira had a job to do. A very important one. She couldn't believe her recklessness. She was embarrassed of how she had spent her day. The Willoughby branch of the Otter Tail County Library had been closed for much too long.

There were books waiting for her. Long, twisting, delicious books on every shelf. Books with proper endings. And if Moira knew anything at all, it was that they needed to be appreciated, they needed to be used. They needed to be read, over and over again. Until her brain was quiet. Until she could see Henry's face once more, blonde and smiling and perfect.

Flatlands

They stopped because Dylan had to pee.

"I told you not to drink so much Diet Coke." Their mom looked over her shoulder into the backseat. "Both of you."

Dylan squirmed underneath his seatbelt at the memory of the enormous fountain pop he begged for at the Kwik Stop in Jamestown. The empty plastic cup taunted him from the floor of the van.

"You should have gone after lunch, I told you," his big sister, Danni, chimed in.

Danni was just thirteen and had the awkward long legs and flat chest to match. She wasn't tall for her age, rather average, but she still towered over Dylan. He would be going into the fourth grade. And while Danni, the soon to be seventh grader, was skinny, her little brother Dylan was short and boxy like their father. Yet brother and sister shared the same distinct green eyes.

The rest area consisted of an A-frame building with a thickly shingled, sloping roof. The structure was uniquely seventies; its dark wood slatted windows could not be of this century. To the right was a grassy expanse surrounded by four signs, stuck in the soil at varying heights. Each sign had the same image, the profile of a white terrier with a red leash rising into nothing.

Danni followed her little brother out of the van. She walked slowly on the paved path, thankful to work her legs and breathe in real air. Her baby blue cotton dress flapped between her knees in the breeze. Dylan ran ahead, his hands cupping his crotch. A woman recognized his distress and stopped to hold the glass door open for him to rush through. Danni watched him nod his head in hurried gratitude and disappear inside.

She passed a group of teenagers, all older than she, in matching purple t-shirts with a gold cross emblazoned on the back, and FARGO TEENS FOR CHRIST! written in block letters on the front. They marched past her toward a school bus pulled up to the curb. The orange bus looked wrong there, in the middle of nowhere, in the middle of summer. Danni never wanted to know what it felt like to sit

---

on the plastic seats and drive across the plains. It was bad enough to endure it the few blocks to her middle school.

A newspaper rack, the old-fashioned kind, was pushed up against the tan stucco on the front of the building next to a spigot that protruded out over a rusty bucket. Danni wondered if people used this spout of cold water to make coffee or clean their armpits or scrub clay from their sandals. The newspaper rack was open; she could see a few thin papers inside. She was compelled to put her hand inside the rusted metal mouth and pull out a flier. It was a map of North Dakota, just a simple one with the highways and big towns marked in black. The shape of the state struck her, how it was nearly a perfect rectangle.

Danni was from Minnesota, a place created by the unpredictable curves of its lakes and rivers. She didn't know a state could be so symmetrical. She had studied the states in school, but she had never fully appreciated the shape of North Dakota on its own. Even I-90 was a near perfect line, cutting North Dakota into two distinct sections. A bright green arrow pointed to a symbol that looked like a crude drawing of a house. It represented a rest stop, the one she stood in. YOU ARE HERE. They were on the left side of the rectangle, close to the thick line that read MONTANA.

Danni's father had promised the drive would become more interesting once they crossed over to Montana. He said there were mountains there and they would drive up and up, until they were on the edge of a precipice, skirting along the flimsy railing in their Toyota.

That supposed high place full of craggy mountain sides and dipping streams seemed alien to Danni now. They were in the flatlands, the plains, where the sky and the land fused together to make a never-ending line. There was only the brown, shingled building jutting from the soil and rising into the cloudless sky as though it had crashed into the endless prairies from above. It looked to be an accident, a mistaken blot on a perfect and symmetrical painting.

Danni was suddenly aware of her presence in this blight on the land; she was no different than the TEENS FOR CHRIST or Dylan who was surely scrubbing his hands in one of the many provided sinks. She had the most bizarre idea that if she wasn't there, if they all weren't there, the plains could restore themselves. She saw an image of the tall grass stretching into thick, snake like vines and scaling up the overhanging roof until the building was green with writhing vegetation. She imagined there would be a growling rumble from far underneath, deep, deep inside the flatlands. And then the insulting structure would be eaten; chewed and swallowed by the dry grass and the red soil until it was underneath with the prairie dogs and the worms.

And then the buffalo would come and trample the ground back into its original smoothness and the perfect rectangle state would be plain once again, even and indefinite.

The map slipped from her fingers and fluttered to the pavement. Danni felt a prickly shudder run through her. Her mind felt used, intruded upon. A channel had been momentarily switched in her brain from the regularly scheduled program, yet she didn't remember touching the remote. She could see the family van and the vague outlines of her parents in the front seats. Although she could not see their expressions she could sense their impatience. She stepped away from the map. One of its corners fluttered madly in the breeze.

"Danni!"

She watched the vibrating paper ripple and move.

It's alive.

"Danni! Danielle!" Dylan held one of the glass entrance doors open with one bony arm. He stretched his head out and waved with his free hand. "Come here!"

Danni tore her gaze away from the map and watched her little brother. As she walked closer, she recognized distress in his eyes.

"What is it? Did you pee your pants?" She hoped she would see a dark stain on his khaki shorts, not because she wanted him to be humiliated, but because she was afraid by the crease in his forehead and the twitch dancing on his top lip.

Dylan shook his head. "Come see this."

She passed through the door and he let it swing shut behind them. The silence struck Danni first. There were no kids jumping from bench to bench and no sound of the air hand dryers blasting from behind the restroom doors.

Dylan pulled her hand and led her around a spinning rack of brochures. There was a bench tucked into an alcove. It looked upon an enormous picture window that showcased the endless prairie before them. There were purple wildflowers hitting the glass in a stilted rhythm.

Alive.

Then she saw the old woman. She sat in the middle of the bench with her back to them, her face toward the plains. Her hair was not the comforting white fluff of grandmothers but rather a faded orange Danni had only previously associated with wiry spaniels. The woman was dressed in a quilted jacket, each square a different sort of geometrical design.

"I think she's dead," Dylan's voice echoed off the cream, brick walls.

Danni looked down at her little brother and frowned. She wanted to ask him why he hadn't just left the bathroom and skipped outside into the sunshine. What had made him turn the corner? Why had he wanted to stay a moment longer in such a silent and ugly place?

"I talked to her and touched her back and she just stayed like that Danni."

She would ask him later why he had touched her. And then she would hit him and yell at him for being so damn stupid. But now she only had the power to swallow the sickness rising in her throat.

Dylan moved toward the figure on the bench and Danni instinctively tried to grab him back. He moved too quickly and she stumbled forward. The sound of her skidding flip flops did not rouse the woman from the bench.

"If she's dead we gotta tell Mom and Dad and then they can call the police," Dylan said.

Her nine-year-old brother's logic was foreign to her ears. She couldn't picture police officers in this room, it wasn't right. She could only think of the other outcomes, the ones that seemed more than possible. She thought of the witch in Hansel and Gretel, she thought of the grass becoming thick living vines, she thought of the flapping map.

Dylan took his small, shaking finger and poked the woman's back. He then pressed his whole fist into the quilted jacket and gave a considerable punch. Danni watched, unbelieving, questioning his strange, misplaced bravery.

The woman was a statue of flesh. Her veiny hands sat lifeless in her lap. Yet her neck was not bent to the side, and her chin didn't sink into her chest. Her wrinkled skin was pink.

"She's not dead," Danni said weakly.

Danni had watched *Night of The Living Dead* on her iPad that summer. Her father had said she could watch any horror movie as long it was in black and white. "Then it won't be too damn gory," he had assured her. She had watched *Psycho* too and one about a giant ant that terrorized a small town. So she had seen what dead bodies looked like, fake ones at least, and at twelve years old she could safely assume that fake dead bodies were modeled after real ones.

"That woman, she's not dead, Dylan, she's not dead."

Somehow she felt more scared. If they had found a dead old lady at a North Dakota rest stop she could see the fluid logic of it, the potential story to tell her friends on the first day of seventh grade. But it was the life, still visible around the lady, in her, that shook Danni's entire frame.

Dylan dropped his hands and wiped both palms on the sides of his shorts as though he had just touched a dead mouse.

Not dead. Alive.

Danni reached out and grabbed Dylan's bony shoulder. "C'mon."

They stepped carefully backward, both watching the specter on the bench. If the woman moved, if she slowly turned her old, creaking neck and revealed a toothy grin, Danni was sure she would die of fear. She thought of *Psycho*'s Mrs. Bates, propped up in the basement, and wished for a harmless old woman like her, all bones and ash.

Dylan wiggled under Danni's tight grasp and ran to the glass doors that were twinkling with sunlight and hope. Danni didn't want to stop looking at the thing with the old lady jacket, but she pushed her legs forward and followed him out into the heat. She fell forward on the pavement and landed on her elbows.

"Stop!" She could feel the sting of the fall on her arms. Her mother would insist on an antiseptic wipe. "Don't tell them." She panted. Air was returning to her lungs in dramatic gasps.

The family van still waited in the lot. But now it was alone. Danni pushed herself up from the ground, feeling wobbly on her feet. She squinted in the complete sunlight. The vast sky was cloudless. Her parents were not in the vehicle. She shaded her eyes with a hand and looked harder, blinking the sun stars from her vision. There were no shadows or movements.

A semi-truck passed on the distant slash of I-90 with a monstrous roar. Danni felt at first what she believed were the truck's reverberations underneath her, in the soil. But the aftershocks continued, pulsating up through her legs and into the pit of her belly with a thundering beat.

Danni's mind was seized again. Images intruded upon her. She could see herself, outside of her body. She was small and insignificant, alone, in the endless plains. There were no cars or rest stops or offending roads slicing into the horizon. Tall, brown grass enveloped her in a scratchy hug and she was at peace. There was nothing, nothing but the flatlands, her flatlands, and she wanted to be that girl in the grass.

Her eyes were her own again. The ground underneath still pounded like an enormous pumping heart, like it was…

Alive.

She needed to run. She needed to go into the prairie. Away from the paved lot with the single van and away from the ugly brown structure with the lady thing inside. Dylan ran behind her, screaming her name and pleading with her to stop. Danni heard the fear in his voice and she wondered if the soil shook his feet too.

There was nothing ahead. She was comforted by the infinity. She ran into thicker grass and it began to tickle her bare arms. She wondered if night came here or if the sun was forever too.

"Danni!" He struggled in the brush behind her. "DANNI!" His voice, scared and young, didn't belong here. She knew this, as she knew the prairie.

She dropped to her knees; the power underneath her was more than she could bear. It made her brain fuzzy and she could sense a takeover of her mind.

The channel changed. She could see the sky was an impossible red. She was outside of her body once more and there was something sharp in her hand, she could feel the weight of it. Her nose was full of a metallic, wretched tang that could only be blood. Danni watched herself in the red grass, stalking him with the sharp thing in her small hand. That girl wanted to hurt him, the red girl who smelled blood.

The picture was gone. The movie was over. Danni was still crouched low. She was uncertain that if there was an actual cutting thing in her hands if she would use it. She thought she might, just to appease the red in her mind.

He caught up to her then. His eyes were wild and confused. He looked at her as though he didn't know her. She wanted to hug him, to pull him down and kiss his head as she had when he was smaller. But she wanted to hurt him, too.

She saw the knife.

It stuck up from the soil as though it had started as a tiny knife seed and had grown into a viable crop. The handle was covered in a messy mound of earth, but the shining metal edge shot up in the air.

He saw it, too.

"Dylan," Danni said softly. "I think," she felt herself move toward the knife, anxious to feel the weight in her palm, just like the red girl had. "I think maybe you should run."

His chest heaved with effort as he watched his sister's trembling hand reach out to the knife buried in the ground.

Danni dropped to her knees and began to claw at the dirt around the sharp thing. She heard her brother make a sort of squeaking gasp before he flew into the high grass and ran.

She was at once disappointed and pleased he had left her alone. She didn't want to do the thing with the knife, yet she had it in her hands now, so it seemed inevitable.

The sky had a palpable heaviness. The wind was picking up, swishing through the grass around her and creating the salty scent of earth. In an instant the sun was blotted out by dark clouds. The light changed into the eerie orange reminiscent of the bright red in her mind picture. Danni could feel the prairie's strength, still beating underneath her, as she made her way back to the building.

They stood near the doors. Her father paced on the sidewalk, his head in his hands. Her mother stood with her arms crossed and her eyes on the horizon. She saw Danni first.

Her mother pointed to her daughter emerging from the prairie and then her father stopped pacing and began to run toward her.

Danni watched as her parent's faces changed. They were relieved as she made her way out of the grass, but as she came closer, as she could hear their breath and their questions, she recognized the fear in their widening pupils and their pale cheeks.

And then she used the sharp thing and they were very scared.

She wanted a rest, and this strange, ugly building was called a rest stop after all. It was going to rain, so she would sit inside. Dylan would get wet out there, she mused. He would be soaked and lost and alone.

Danni found the bench and took a seat. She noticed the old lady thing had red on her, streaked in crusty ragged lines on the front of her quilted jacket. Danni hadn't looked at her front before. But that was okay because Danni had red on her too. Her hands were slippery red. But she was thinking of a brilliant, regal purple now, the shade of the wildflowers that tickled the window in front of them.

The flowers that seemed, somehow, someway, alive.

Meg Hafdahl

Guts

I have a scar on my belly. It's a wretched, milky white line that crawls up from the bottom of my abdomen until it meets my bellybutton. When I saw it for the first time, still cloudy with drugs, I was struck with how deep the divot of the cut went into my formally unblemished stomach. I remembered how my husband kissed my belly once, long before the surgery, and said he loved the smoothness of my skin, all over. This memory made tears trickle down my cheeks. But I couldn't sob in my hands or pull in a hitching breath, because it would hurt my guts too much.

That surgery was a while ago, after we got married but before we had Josie. When I was pregnant I would note the taut nature of my scar as it expanded with my body. Sometimes I wondered if it would be strained too much by the growing child inside and finally split open to let my insides spill out on to my shoes.

That didn't happen. Instead I had a healthy baby girl and went back to waiting for my guts to betray me in another, less showy way. They did, of course. They always have. My first memories are of hospital waiting rooms, hushed, worried voices, a pain in my stomach and hot vomit on my chin. I grew up snacking on Tums. I knew nothing but a bloated uncomfortableness.

Now, I visit the hospital every six weeks to silence my guts. I'm there for about four hours, maybe more if the nurses are swamped. They offer me a warm blanket and crackers and I can watch cable, a break from Josie's strict regimen of PBS cartoons. I get a bed, which is nice; they give a bed to people like me and the ones with cancer receiving chemo. I'm thankful I'm not there to get chemo. My IV medicine is an immunosuppressant, it forces my system to stop attacking my intestines. Otherwise my body will eat my guts. And I never want to feel that sensation again. It's like hot coals. You can taste the pain on your tongue. You can taste the fear too.

So I was curled up in my bed, in a small room with a window overlooking downtown. Snow swirled. The IV was stuck in my hand this time. I had given up trying to type emails on my laptop. The needle hurt and the cords wanted to twist up like crazy. HGTV was on but was hard to hear over the beeps and clatters coming from the nurse's desk right outside my door. I had about an hour remaining and I wanted to doze, just wanted to lose myself in my pillow. Because once the IV was pulled out, I would have to instantly return to the world. The healthy world. Out there I have to forget about my guts. I'm a mother.

"Still good?" The snack cart guy poked his head in my door. He's older, a small man with wisps of white hair sticking out of both ears.

I nodded. "I finished off the graham crackers."

"Want more?" Snack Guy always speaks with a soft, slow voice like I'm a caged animal he's trying to keep calm. "I've got fruit snacks now."

"No, thank you." I turned my head and looked out into the snow.

We were eight floors up, so there were no people to see, only frosted windows and blowing flakes. I heard him push his squeaky cart past my door and on to the next lucky patient. I began to drift off. My head felt heavy and I let my eyelids close. The din of the hospital created a sort of predictable white noise, a comforting oasis from real life. I heard the familiar beeps of empty IV bags and kinked cords. The nurses paced back and forth on soft heeled shoes. Just as I let myself fall into the welcoming blackness, a strange sound pulsed through the air. It was powerful and deafening. I opened my eyes and watched as the door to my little hospital room swung shut as though it were pushed by a defiant ghost. An alarm trilled all around me. I sat up and pushed a pile of warm blankets off my legs. I still had my jeans on and my ankle length boots. We didn't have to wear gowns in the infusion wing. I carefully pulled out the electrical cord anchoring my IV to the wall. My medicine continued to drip into my veins as I pulled the trolley behind me.

My body trembled with relief when I was able to pull my door open and walk out into the nurse's station. The wing consisted of twelve single rooms arranged in a circle around the main desk. There were two bathrooms and several supply closets too, as well as a warmer for blankets that looked oddly like an enlarged toaster oven. There was a row of comfy chairs, pillowed recliners, for those needing a short infusion, an hour or less. All the patient doors had slammed shut like mine. A worried face popped out of room 8-09. She was perhaps mid-forties and her head was shiny bald. She looked at me from across the circular room with anxious, darting eyes. I just shrugged in response, keeping a steady hand on my trolley.

The alarm continued to pulse overhead. Red lights flashed in unison in the corners of the main room. Nurse Jessica, barely old enough to visit a bar, flew out of room 8-04 with a string of gauze flapping behind her. She was pudgy and generally a slow and relaxed sort, who often yawned while taking my blood pressure. But now Jessica zipped to the main desk with incredible speed, wrenching up the phone and dialing frantically. As she screamed into the receiver, trying to be heard over the sound of the alarm, I noticed the doors to the waiting room were shut too. They were white metal and large enough to be mistaken for the gates of a fortress. I wondered what would happen to someone standing in the way when the alarm sounded and they swiftly shut. They would surely knock me down.

"YOU THINK IT'S A FIRE OR WHAT?" Snack Guy shouted over the noise. He lingered in the hall, his liver spotted hands gripping the cart.

I just shook my head, anxious now for an answer. It worried me he was a volunteer and he hadn't been trained on such things.

Nurse Alan came out of one of the supply closets, a fresh IV bag in his hand. He strolled past me and gaping Snack Guy on his way to a patient room. He nodded a hello, his neck tattoos visibly creeping out of his blue scrubs. His cool strut made me feel a bit better.

The sound stopped as abruptly as it had started. The red lights flashed another beat and they stopped too.

Jessica set down the phone and cracked each of her knuckles. I waited until she was finished to speak.

"Is everything okay?" My voice sounded far away within my ringing ears.

Jessica forced a thin smile. "Should be over soon, they said it was nothing."

"Isn't it already over?" Snack Guy still had a death grip on his cart, like he was afraid it was going to roll away.

The young nurse cracked her wrists. "Well, we're still locked in," she gestured to the enormous doors to our unit. I saw then that there were no handles, it was more like a wall than a door. "But it'll open soon."

"I hope so," I said. "I have to pick up my daughter from school."

Jessica nodded. She looked down and gave her attention to some pink papers on the desk. Snack Guy waited a beat and then began to take another turn around the circle. I pushed my door open with my free hand until it clicked into the doorstop. I rolled my trolley back to its spot and climbed back into bed with effort. My medicine doesn't make me sick, but it does make me tired. As I shifted around to get comfortable my IV began to beep. I was done.

Alan answered my nurse light. He was cheery as ever, asking about Josie.

"How's kindergarten? Does she have friends yet?" He used a wet antiseptic cloth to wipe some dried blood around my IV site.

"Yeah, she and this girl Vienna are inseparable. It's really cute." I looked away as he pulled the needle from my hand.

Alan smiled, sincerely, as he bandaged me up. "Geez, they grow fast. Hey can I see a picture? I don't think you've showed me one since that one of her in that little Hanukkah thing, that little play."

I gladly produced a picture of Josie on my phone. She was decorating my birthday cake and had yellow frosting in her eyelashes.

"She looks like you." Alan remarked. We got that a lot. Both Josie and I have long black hair and thick, distinctive eyebrows. But she has her father's piercing green eyes thankfully, not my muddy hazel ones.

"Yeah, say, that door is going to open soon right? I mean, I need to pick her up."

He stopped and stared out into the snow. "Oh sure…probably, but maybe you should text your husband in case, you know, if we're cutting it close."

Yes, of course. Jack could do it. I picked up my phone from the bedside table and wrote a message.

"Might as well hang out here in your bed till it opens. I'll let you know if you miss it." Alan rubbed at a tattoo on his wrist. This one was of a snake, coiled and ready to pounce.

I slept. There was no bothersome itch in my hand now, no reason for nurses to come in and out. So I slept hard. When I woke to the sound of the yelling, I immediately could sense the change of light outside. It was dinnertime, my belly echoed this sentiment with a grumble. There was barely any sunlight left, just a line of pink light really. I looked at the TV next, wondering if the yelling came from an emphatic home buyer on House Hunters, but no. The shrill voice was just outside at the nurse's station. And whoever she was, she was mad. I would peek and see what the commotion was about, but first I checked my texts.

Still there?
What's up?

Nothing on news about a lockdown.
Feeding Josie pizza, hope that's okay ☺
???

They were all from Jack.

"...I was supposed to be here for an hour! I told my daughter I'd be here an HOUR!" The woman's angry voice filled my room. At first I thought it might be the woman with cancer, the one with the bald head, but it was an older woman, tiny and brittle, slamming her wrinkled fist on the counter. Nurse Jessica watched with raised eyebrows. She looked as though she might laugh at the buzzing, little woman.

Alan walked smoothly across the floor and patted the old woman's bony shoulder. Her face was red with rage, which only made the deep grooves around her eyes more prominent. Her lips were carefully lined in a shade of plum and her nails were perfectly manicured.

"You can go ahead and take one of the empty rooms Mrs. Folwell, then you can rest." Alan, with his muscular arms and thick torso, looked like a giant next to elderly Mrs. Folwell.

"I don't want to rest." She spat through her plum lips. "I want to get OUT OF HERE!"

Alan and Jessica shared a glance.

"The door is still shut?" I inquired from the safety of my door frame. "It's been almost three hours."

"Precisely!" Mrs. Folwell trumpeted. "My daughter must be sick with worry, she's just on the other side of that door and I can't even speak to her. This is ridiculous! I have never, in all my life, been subjected to such treatment! I want to speak to someone on the phone, a hospital administrator, someone with some authority!"

I skulked back into my room and shut the door. Mrs. Folwell's emphatic protestations continued, although now thankfully muffled behind the door. I felt something in my gut, not pain, but worry and an inexplicable sickness. I called Jack.

"Hey, what's going on Kelly?" He said after two and a half rings.

"I don't know, I don't know." Tears were threatening to fall. I took a deep breath and sniffed them away. "There's still nothing on the news? No reason? Something that happened, like maybe a stolen infant? I heard they go on lockdown for..."

"No." Jack interrupted. "No news, can't the nurses tell you anything?"

I explained that there was an angry old lady demanding answers and not getting any.

Jack said I was breaking up.

There was static on his side, too. I could hear a few staccato words, something about Josie and her bath, but then we were disconnected. I tried to phone back, but the call failed.

The sickness rose in my belly and I felt the first prickle of my nervous sweats.

I left my room and found a few people milling about in the central nurse's area. Alan was attending to purple Mrs. Folwell. She looked as though she would explode from all the injustice. He settled her back into one of the recliners.

Snack Guy sat a few seats away from her. He was nibbling on a bag of his own pretzels. I wondered what the policies said about that. His cart was planted firmly between his knees.

A teenage girl sat on the hard tiled floor across from the impenetrable doors. She was African American and had on a hoodie marked East High with a pair of skinny red jeans. She had headphones tucked in her ears and a similar bandage like mine around her hand.

I could see the woman with cancer was still hooked up to her IV in her room. Her TV was shut off and she stared forward, a kidney shaped vomit pan sitting in her lap.

Nurse Jessica was in the room next to mine, talking in hushed whispers with a middle aged man in overalls. His name, Rick, was stitched in cursive over the pocket on his chest. There were some grease stains on his legs, where he surely wiped dirty hands.

"Excuse me?" I poked my head into the room. I was immediately conscious of how quickly Jessica and Rick stopped speaking and took a few steps away from each other and the empty bed. "At the risk of sounding like that old lady, I just, I just wanted to know if you heard anything? If anyone has told you why we're locked in here?"

Jessica shook her head. "No, um, there's nothing to worry about. I'm sure it will be over soon." She flashed a fake, toothy smile. She moved past me, back to her post at the enormous, circular desk. Her plump cheeks were crimson and her eyelids fluttered like a pair of trapped butterflies.

"Probably a malfunction is all." Rick in the overalls boomed. His deep voice trembled on the last word. He picked up a plastic tool box from the empty patient bed and began to organize his tools with work-worn hands.

A rumble echoed inside my belly once more. I thought of the pizza Jake and Josie had shared. It would have been nice to have been trapped inside a Pizza Hut, or perhaps a movie theater with bags of hot buttered popcorn. Not here in a hospital, trapped with all the sickness inside.

I trailed around the circular desk, watching as Alan left simmering Mrs. Folwell to attend to Bald Woman. The nurse signal binged above her door.

Snack Guy saw me coming and smiled with the anticipation of being able to actually help. "Hungry?" He brushed pretzel crumbs off his lap. I almost told him about the crystals of salt clinging to his grey moustache but stopped myself. He didn't look like he would care too much. He maintained his smile, but his eyes were scared, unsure.

I helped myself to a strawberry granola bar, the last one. I eyed the old woman pressed into a recliner as I unwrapped my snack. She panted like a dog. I couldn't help but think she resembled an eternally anxious Chihuahua, with her spiky frosted hair and claw like manicure. I wondered when Alan would break out the sedatives from the medicine supply closet. I could use a taste, too; I was wired after my nap.

"How many of us?" I chewed on my snack.

Snack Guy considered the old woman, a few seats down, and then whispered; "Me, you, her," he gave a slight nod toward the recliner. "There's Ms. Good, she's the youth." He said "youth" like it was a dirty word, a nasty moniker that couldn't fit properly in his mouth. "The two nurses of course, and Rick, he's maintenance."

"And the woman, the bald one." I offered.

"Right, so eight of us, just eight."

"Is that usual?" I threw my trash in a nearby bin and then settled in next to him. Mrs. Folwell, to my left, sighed and heaved dramatically. I forced my eyes to stay off of her. Looking at her nervous, bony face would my make my throat dry up.

Snack Guy scrunched his face in confusion. A few salt flakes fell onto his lip.

"I mean, it seems like there are usually more people, you know, more patients?"

He nodded. "It's a slow day I guess."

Ms. Good slid past me, a cloud of fruity perfume following close behind. She took a bag of saltines off the cart wordlessly, her ears still stuffed with headphones. We watched as she opened her treat with her teeth and then kneeled on a couch pushed against a large window. She kept her back to us and pressed her forehead against the glass. Her patent leather boots moved to the beat of the music we couldn't hear.

Ms. Good was straining to see what was happening down below, where the road curved into the hospital's main entrance. Her young face glowed with the blue of the street lights. Her mother must be worried, I thought. Or maybe her mother was hardened now, after whatever illness ravaged her daughter and sent her up here to the eighth floor with people like me, people who have angry guts. And people like Bald Woman, grasping her vomit bowl. What sickness had betrayed such a beautiful girl?

"Oh Jesus." Her tinny voice could barely be heard over the sputtering of Mrs. Folwell. "Oh Jesus!" She repeated, pulling the cords from her ears. They tangled into her curly, brown hair, but she left them there. "Come look!"

Snack Guy jumped up first, letting his cart slam into the wall with a hollow thud. He cupped his hands around his eyes and looked out the window, his chin squashed into his chest in order to see far down.

"What? What is all that?"

I didn't want to look.

I waited for an explanation. I pulled the cuffs of my sweater over my fingers and rubbed my face. I was cold and tired and I didn't, I couldn't taste fear again. Not ever again.

They were statues, still pressed against the glass.

"What?" I finally choked.

Ms. Good swiveled around and plopped onto the couch. The earphones still hung limply in her hair. Her lips made a serious dash across her face. She didn't speak.

"Everyone's leaving," Snack Guy kept his eyes on the window. Now there were red lights illuminating his wispy face. "In buses and ambulances, there are some cop vehicles I think."

The girl bobbed her head. "They're running. Some of them are running."

I couldn't imagine the chaos. Not in the snowy dark. We couldn't hear any of it, no screeching tires or ambulance wails.

"Check your phone, check the news." I suggested. My feet were now curled up underneath me. I couldn't. I just couldn't watch the scene unfold below.

Snack Guy was shaking. His hands tapped against the glass.

The young girl pulled a bright yellow smart phone from the front pocket of her hooded sweatshirt. "Yahoo says nothing." She clicked a button. "Local says nothing, there's nothing."

"The hospital is evacuating and it's not on the news? We're trapped up here and no one knows why?" It was Mrs. Folwell. She was vibrating in her seat. Her jaws clenched together. She stood on stick legs and shuffled over to the window. They were all there now. They watched the world below.

"My name is Kelly." I told their backside. Even the youth, as she titled, turned her face back toward the lights.

"My name is Mackenzie Good." She said into the glass. "And my mom is getting McDonald's for me. Or I mean, she was. It's cold now, and she won't answer my texts."

"I'm Mort," Snack Guy stepped back from the window. "I volunteer every Thursday." He would always be Snack Guy to me.

"What are you in here for Kelly?" Mackenzie moved away from the window too. She fiddled with the phone in her hand.

"Oh, I'm just here to get my meds." Obviously, I thought, as I rubbed my sore hand.

I wanted to ask Mackenzie about her illness, but I stopped myself. I didn't want to know, it seemed too real, too scary to think of such a young girl being sick.

Mrs. Folwell stepped forward. "I have osteoporosis in my hip, and I was supposed to be here just for forty-five minutes, in and out." She seemed to be speaking to no one, just the walls and chairs around her. We were all furniture to her, featureless and forgotten. "And now my daughter can't reach me." She took in a wobbly breath. "I need to use the restroom," she finished randomly.

Mackenzie rolled her eyes in the dramatic, indulgent way only teenagers can.

"Your mom's not texting you back?" I asked as the old woman left for the toilet. I was glad they had all removed themselves from the window. It made me feel better to see their faces.

Mackenzie shook her head. She jumped over and got in the recliner next to me. "Here." She scrolled through a line of texts, one sided, from her to her mother. Despite the desperate exclamation points and capital letters, there were no answers.

"My phone wasn't working either. It can't dial out." Snack Guy produced an old flip phone from his slack pockets. "And it's dead now."

A high pitched squeak. It reminded me of a mouse, desperate for its life, trapped under a cat's paw. The squeak came several more times, intensifying in sound and length each time. Mackenzie was the first to jump up. The headphones finally fell from her curls and skimmed the linoleum. She absently stuffed them into her pocket. We lived in the silence, waiting for another squeak, or even a familiar beep.

"Mrs. Folwell?" Nurse Alan knocked on the bathroom door. The old woman didn't answer. "Pull the cord by the toilet. It will unlock the door ma'am."

Nothing.

Jessica sidled in next to Alan, her considerable rump swaying back and forth. She rapped on the door with both hands. "Mrs. Folwell? Lydia….did you fall?"

Snack Guy and Mackenzie joined the action, circling around the two nurses. Even the bald woman's curiosity was piqued. She pulled her chemo trolley behind her into the chaos. She gave me a similarly anxious look as when the doors had locked. But now the dark crescents under her eyes were deeper.

"Damn woman worked herself into a tizzy and fainted," Rick, the handyman, said, leaning against the wall. He took a pistachio out of his chest pocket and unshelled it with one finger. He popped the nut into his mouth and sighed as though he were sufficiently bored. Rick was probably the same age as Snack Guy, early sixties, but he had assuredly lived a harder life. His pale blue eyes were uninterested and his brow was permanently furrowed.

Jessica retrieved a key from some secretive place and jammed it into the knob.

"Everyone give us some space." Hulking Alan pushed the air around the spectators. Bald Woman didn't move. She kept her prime spot, holding the trolley carefully as it was connected to a port in her chest. I had a PICC line once, a long cord embedded into my chest connected to an IV machine on wheels. I bled buckets when they had put it in. I remember how cautious I was when moving, just like the Bald Woman. I had nightmares of it being yanked out by an errant foot or hand. How it would rip my chest open.

I remained in my seat as Jessica heaved the bathroom door open. I was holding my knees to my chin, unwilling to stretch my neck and take a peek. I just couldn't. I knew something bad was coming. Just as I knew when my sickness was coming back, full force.

Mackenzie screamed first, shrill and unending. I hoped maybe she had just seen a frail old woman on the toilet and that was frightful enough.

But then Snack Guy knelt on the shiny floor and began to vomit in a rather tidy pile. I buried my face into my hands.

"WHAT THE FUCK?" Alan roared. I could hear his panicky breath as he entered the bathroom.

I could hear Jessica skidding on her nurse shoes too. Bald Woman didn't make a sound though. Nothing could scare her. There was something comforting about that notion.

I could make out only a small sliver of light between my clenched legs. Suddenly, as Mackenzie's high pitched wails continued to trill in my ears, the light flashed off. I raised my head no more than an inch, taking in the darkness. All the overhead fluorescents were dead. The numerous exit signs were still a fuzzy red. I could hear a series of mechanical clicks in between the screams and the coughs. The generators were taking over.

It was dark, but there were emergency lights, frosted blue, lining the walls. One shone from the bathroom where Alan had disappeared inside. Jessica stood outside the door, her ruddy cheek pressed into the frame. She cracked each of her knuckles and then began again, pulling at each finger until it satisfied her with a snap.

Mackenzie finally closed her mouth. Fat tears flowed. She huddled into the seat next to mine, sniffling.

"The old lady…" she trailed off. Her face was pale and ghostlike in the blue light.

Snack Guy was actually cleaning up his vomit. He had produced a pair of latex gloves and a plastic bag in the dim light. It was sort of impressive really.

"We have to get that door open. We have to pry it open." Rick was no longer lazing against the wall. Now, clearly agitated by what he had seen in the bathroom, he was making his way across the circle with his toolbox, heading toward the doors with no handles.

Mackenzie surprised me by taking my hand. "You have to see Kelly, you have to look at her."

No. No. I couldn't.

"I just think I'll sit here." I said. As though that was a decent plan.

"Kelly," Mackenzie swallowed. "That old lady is dead…"

"Okay." I cut her off.

"Something," the young girl's voice hitched. "Something did that to her."

I shook my head.

Rivulets of sweat ran down from both my armpits. I couldn't.

Snack Guy remained on his knees. "Her body is ripped up." He said matter-of-factly. "There's blood on the ceiling." He still spoke in that careful, lilting voice he used when offering a straw for my soda.

I wished I had a sweatshirt like Mackenzie, one with a hood to cover my head.

"I think you need to see," Mackenzie stared forward, out into the still swirling snow.

Alan exited the bathroom. His blue scrubs were covered in black, no, no it wasn't black. Even in the dim light I could make out the red.

He was sweating too, his forehead was slick and his eyes bulged like his sinewy arms. Jessica watched him silently.

"Your pagers? What about your phones? Or the main phone?" Snack Guy was standing now, holding his bag of vomit like a clutch purse.

"They don't work, they haven't for hours," Jessica said, nibbling on her thumbnail.

Alan shushed her.

"This isn't normal," Bald Woman spoke. She was staring at the aberration in the bathroom.

"No shit." Mackenzie's chin trembled.

Jessica pushed Alan's back. "We have to get out of here! WE HAVE TO!"

Alan swiveled around and grabbed his fellow nurse's wrists. "She has no hip Jessica. It's fucking gone." He breathed into Jessica's face. Her marble eyes grew wider and her mouth formed a perfect O.

"What?" Snack Guy plopped his bag on the counter and stepped toward the bathroom. "What did you say?"

"Something ate clean through her hip." Bald Woman rubbed at her hairless brow with one hand. The other, pink with strain, held her trolley steady.

I shook my head. "No, no, no."

"Who did this?" Snack Guy stood with hands on his hips and his lips jutting out under his moustache. Like he was damn Hercule Poirot here to apprehend a guilty British playboy.

"None of us." Alan let go of his grip on Jessica. She remained in the same position, her arms bound with invisible rope.

"And how do you know that? Why say that?" Snack Guy actually raised his voice.

"Because something with sharp teeth, or claws, chewed up that horrible woman in less than three minutes." Bald Woman pointed into the bathroom with a long, skinny finger.

"Why her hip?" Mackenzie was on the edge of her chair, ready to jump or run in an instant.

No. I couldn't say it. It was too horrible. I kept it to myself.

I finally stood, on Jello legs, and attempted to walk in the opposite direction of the bathroom. I would just take the long way around the circle to avoid the bloody hipless body of Mrs. Folwell.

"It was her left one," Alan mumbled to himself as he dropped into one of the chairs. Maybe he knew too.

I was taking steps to get to my room. I wanted my phone in my hand. Maybe I could text Jack and he could get to me somehow. He could get some sort of rope or pulley that would get up to the eighth floor and save me. I could break a window and then we could all get out. The cold air would feel so good on my face.

I wanted to ask Alan, or even Snack Guy, to come with me to my room. Maybe even Bald Woman, she seemed sufficiently bad ass. But before I could speak, before words could form in my mind I saw there was a lump next to the doors.

Don't Kelly. Don't turn your head.

Rick was dead. Aside from a few calm looking bodies in their open caskets, I had never seen a dead person before. But I knew Rick was dead. He was on his stomach and the contents of his tool box were spread out beside his head.

"Uh….uh….uh…" I managed. Bald Woman was standing the closest and noticed my distress first.

"What is it girl?"

The way she said girl crawled up my spine. As though I wasn't a thirty four year old mother who had gone through the indignity of having a section of my intestines removed. As though I didn't know pain.

I pointed. It was all I could do. They all caught wind of what was happening. Alan got to the body first. He rolled the dead man over. His tongue was clearly gone.

No. I can't.

His eyes were open and his mouth was gnawed on, his lips were in bloody shreds. I made myself believe it was wax. It was just a wax man, not a real one. I felt myself pulled to the floor by an invisible force. My butt hit the linoleum so hard my teeth chattered.

A set of fuzzy slippers appeared next to me. The Bald Woman's. Mackenzie was right up next to the body. She didn't scream this time, but her lips were chalky white in the blue glow.

Alan checked for a pulse.

"We can't be alone…no one can be alone." Snack Guy's voice from somewhere.

"Was he sick?" I said through the thick fear in my throat. "Did he have something wrong with him?" I turned to Nurse Jessica. She was hovering behind me.

"I mean he, yeah, he chewed tobacco." Jessica bent her neck to the side until it gave a subtle crack. "He just found out he has mouth cancer."

"Oh my God." Alan stood. "Mrs. Folwell had osteoporosis."

"In her hip," Mackenzie chimed in.

My guts. I held my belly. I could feel the craggy scar underneath my sweater.

A clatter came from behind the nurse's station. A plastic medicine bottle rolled out from behind the tall desk. It smacked into Mackenzie's boot with obvious force.

She hiccupped in surprise.

"One...two...three...four..." Snack Guy pointed to each of the living. He then patted his own chest. "Five."

"WHO'S THERE?" Alan bellowed. A bulging vein appeared in his clenched jaw. The black ink coiling up his neck vibrated and changed in the dim light.

He started toward the noise. Bald Woman was beginning to understand. Her tired face began to awaken. She had been beautiful before the cancer, I could see that now as the realization flushed her thin cheeks.

She raised her free hand and grabbed Alan's massive bicep. Her strength startled both herself and the nurse. They shared a long glance, her hand still gripping into his flesh. "Alan, are you sick?"

Alan shook his head. He carefully brushed her hand from his arm. "I have to see who it is."

I turned away.

Everyone stood around me as I remained on the floor. Each foot crept forward to see. Mackenzie tip-toed toward the desk. They wanted to see what was behind there. They needed to know what made the folders fall on the floor and the pencil roll.

I couldn't.

I was forced to look at Rick. He was slumped against the doors, sticky blood pooled underneath his head. Something had chewed up his tongue before he could even scream. We hadn't heard a struggle or a single kick. Mrs. Folwell had only emitted a few desperate squeaks while her hip was removed. Whichever direction I looked there was too much reality, too much. I squeezed my eyes shut and cradled my head.

A symphony of breaths, some heavy and shaking, some shallow and hesitant. I wished for cotton balls to stuff in my ears.

Mackenzie's scream, now familiar, sliced through the infusion wing. It echoed eerily against the walls.

I pressed my eyelids together even tighter, until I could see strange bursts of light, like a kaleidoscope in my own personal darkness.

"SHIT!" Alan screamed.

"Get it! GET IT!" Snack Guy demanded.

A door slammed. I could feel the swish of air on my cheek.

"KELLY!" It was Mackenzie. "KELLY! MOVE!"

I almost didn't. For a moment I was sure this was not my life. That I was a detached party, perhaps someone watching a horror movie unfold.

This is not happening.

But then came the skittering behind my back. It sounded at first like a dog trying to find purchase on a slippery floor. Yet it was fast and determined. Gaining toward me. I jumped up. And then I looked. Not because I wanted to, no. I looked because I couldn't believe this was really happening.

At first, when I saw the thing coming toward me, I thought it was one of Josie's toys. She has this stuffed cat that is soft on the outside but hard and mechanical on the inside. It has a pink remote Josie can control easily. Sometimes it will come into the kitchen and walk about awkwardly under my feet while I make dinner. It scared me once when I was on the toilet when it shot by the bathroom door like some deranged living cat.

But it wasn't Lily with pink bows and orange fur crawling across the hospital floor. It was faster and smaller. Just a tiny bit smaller than a mechanical cat, or a real one. What I noticed first were the hands. Hands like a human, but with claws on the ends of the fingers. The talon hands were outstretched while the clawed feet dashed toward me.

It was so small and ugly, I almost laughed.

But as it came closer I felt the need to run. It's black, beady eyes were studying me. It was looking at my middle, straight at where my scar was under a bit of fabric.

It wanted my guts.

I grabbed my stomach like a pregnant woman and ran to the row of recliners. I crawled up onto the top of one and began to kick my feet wildly.

Mackenzie was still screaming. Alan arrived as the thing turned the corner and started for the chairs. It was fleshy. There were rolls of skin on its bulbous back. It had teeth. It had a lot of teeth. I couldn't stop looking at it now. It had to be fake. It couldn't be real.

It leapt on springy back legs and nearly made it onto the recliner next to me. It panted with exertion. Alan had a mop in his hands. I'm not sure when he grabbed it, but I watched in satisfaction as he hit the thing with the handle. There was a squishy thud. Alan hit again and again. Its insides were squirting onto the floor. Red blood. Red like ours.

Its mouth reminded me of Rick's bloody lips. It was human-like in shape, but deformed somehow. The sharp teeth stuck out at every angle as Alan smashed it into the floor.

Mackenzie was actually holding Snack Guy up. He was slipping in her grasp, his eyes rolled back into his head.

Jessica stood on the nurse's desk like a woman who had just encountered a distasteful rodent. She was as still as a statue. Bald Woman was gone.

"Where…." I couldn't produce anymore words. I just coughed and slumped down into the chair.

Alan stopped. Sweat lined his forehead. The thing was dead. We stayed like that for some time.

"No one is coming for us." Mackenzie finally let Snack Guy fall to the floor. She tried to protect his head. "He's fainted is all."

"Your phone?" Alan motioned toward the teenager. She shook her head.

Another one came then, as I somehow knew it would.

It was just as ugly, wrinkled and gnashing its yellow teeth. Mackenzie's panic was evident as she watched it come close. She jumped up on the desk, her feet unsteady on a pile of folders. Jessica clung to her. They held each other, watching the little monster down below.

Alan clutched the mop. He was holding the rag end while the bloody handle rested on the floor. We watched the thing stop at Snack Guy's ear. It actually sniffed the clump of white ear hair with its warty nose.

Then it stopped.

It was a fleshy ball with teeth just like its dead friend. It ignored the unconscious man and began to scratch at the desk, trying to figure out how to get up to the women. How to get to Mackenzie. It was thinking. That was the scariest thing of all. It was considering and taking in the challenge. I grabbed my belly tighter, thinking of its claws. I thought of it finding me, of opening me up and slicing through my skin to gnaw on my insides. It would pull my intestines out like festive streamers and I would watch it happen.

Alan began to creep up behind the thing, his makeshift weapon ready. It didn't seem to hear him, in fact it didn't seem to have anything resembling ears on its pocked, greenish pale skin.

Alan raised the mop and brought it down like a lumberjack wielding an axe. The thing split open in a spray of blood. It didn't have the chance to make a sound of surprise or fear. I wondered what kind of noises a creature like that would make. My stomach churned.

"NOOOO!" It was Bald Woman behind her patient room door. "NOOO! You SHITS!"

Alan, always ready to protect, raced toward the closed door. He swung it open with one hand, still holding his trusty mop in the other.

She was standing on the bed, and she was holding the lift button. She had raised the bed as high as possible. Her chemo cord was still attached to the trolley. I could see only her knees down from my place in the chair. Her slippers had fallen off.

There were dozens of them on the floor. They were fighting to get to her. They didn't care about muscular Alan in the doorway. He was like Snack Guy. Not tasty I suppose. He watched in horror as they scrambled to eat her cancer.

And then the ceiling gave way. I couldn't see it bulge and crack from where I sat, but there was an incredible crash. I could read on Jessica and Mackenzie's face that it was not good.

The ceiling above Bald Woman was a gaping hole, one full of the things, the fleshy things. They streamed out, I could see that much, and they were thrashing about on her bed in the debris. She threw them off. She pushed her bare heel into their teeth and kicked. She was amazing.

Alan used his mop. But before he did, before he charged into that room of those hideous things, he looked back over his shoulder at us. "GET OUT! GO!" He screamed.

One of them had caught on to his plan and was chomping toward him. Perhaps they would bite him to protect themselves, or maybe he did have something inside him like the rest of us sickies, a time bomb they wanted to eat.

Mackenzie looked at me. She searched my eyes for an answer. I wanted to tell her that I couldn't. I couldn't. We would just cover our heads and wait for the pain.

Bald Woman ripped one of the things from her shoulder and threw it at the wall. "AHHH!" She wiped at dripping sweat on her forehead as she screamed, "EAT SHIT YOU UGLY TROLL!"

Alan charged into the room, knee deep in the horrible things.
What if I could?

"We have to break the window," I said. I stood up as if controlled
by some authority I had never known. I was not myself; I was someone
else now, someone who could accept, who could adapt.

"We're eight floors up," Jessica shivered.

"Well we don't have a choice." My heart slammed inside my chest.
"Those things are going to come out here and they are going to eat us."

I found an errant trolley, perhaps the one I had been strung up to
mere hours ago and rolled it over to the window behind the chairs.

Mackenzie dropped from the desk and came to help me. She was
brave. We heaved the metal device up onto our shoulders and then
crashed into the window. A hairline crack appeared. We did it again.

Jessica's nasally voice whined as we worked. "We'll fall," she said.
"The glass won't break, Oo it will and we'll get cut up and they will
smell our blood. We'll fall, right down to the ground," she whined. "We
can't."

I wanted to slap her. Mackenzie was getting weak behind me. We
pushed.

I could hear Alan swinging and crashing and killing those things.
But he sounded weak too. I couldn't hear Bald Woman. But I knew she
couldn't be dead. She was too strong.

The window crumpled finally, shattering glass onto the recliners
and out into the snowy night. I looked down. There were no more
ambulances or buses at the main entrance. Downtown was oddly quiet.
There were no sirens in the swish of freezing air.

When I looked back, Jessica had a pile of blankets in her hands.
She had dropped from the desk and was actually helping.

"Tie 'em together," Mackenzie whispered.

I wasn't sure if those things could hear or not. I saw some dead
and wounded ones scattered in the doorway. But there were more. I
could sense them in the walls now, scratching to get out. Scratching to
get to my guts.

Snack Guy remained a heap on the floor. I couldn't worry about
him now. He was safe. I tied a blanket around a pillar to anchor it and
then we all began to tie the blankets together. There was not enough.
Not even after the pile of them from the warmer.

"Look!" Mackenzie had pushed our escape blanket ladder out of
the window and was watching it swing in the wind. "We just have to
make it to that."

A window cleaner's pulley was abandoned a few floors down. I didn't know they even bothered to clean windows in the winter. But I didn't care. The wooden structure was a bit to the right. We would have to swing ourselves onto it.

Jessica joined us at the open window. We were all shaking in the cold and with the realization we would have to climb down. I felt that familiar fear trying to take over, the sensation that always made me hide rather than face reality.

I didn't let it in, because I have faced worse. I'm angry. I'm angry that I'm sick. It pervades every happiness, it corrodes every hope.

But they are my guts. Screwed up and wrong, hateful even. They are my guts. I harness the anger.

Mackenzie went first. She looked back at the things, piling high to get to Bald Woman and Alan, and then swung her legs out into the cold night. I watched her begin the descent. She smiled as she climbed down.

"Now you," I said, pulling Jessica to the window's edge.

"Oh hell no." She watched Mackenzie ease down the blanket rope. "I can't."

"You can. You have to."

"They won't eat me." She shook her head. "They only eat the bad stuff right?"

The creatures were starting to erupt from every room, a plague of them, and I couldn't wait. She stayed.

I followed Mackenzie. She slithered down the blankets like an agile cat. I clung to the fabric with unsure hands. I didn't think of the road beneath.

"I have psoriasis." She yelled into the windy night. "They want my skin I think."

"Well, they can't have it!" I yelled back. The blanket flapped in the icy breeze.

I looked up to see if Jessica changed her mind. But instead of her face peering down to watch us there were hundreds of those things. They were crawling on the window sill and bashing against the cut glass. Then they began to fall, one at first, and then a group of them, falling past us and landing with a sickening splat on the road below. At least they couldn't fly.

Mackenzie screamed when one of them whizzed right past her nose on the way down. "What...what about you?" Mackenzie was talking to try to calm herself. I could barely hear her below me but it felt good to have her there.

"I have Crohn's disease," I said it. I never said it to a stranger before. "They want my intestines."

"That fucking sucks," she snorted.

"Yeah, yeah you know it really does." We were nearly there.

Mackenzie swung the end of our escape rope, so she could hook a foot onto the washer's platform. She got it on the first try. I was about three blankets behind her and my stomach was bubbling in panic.

As she let go and steadied herself on the wood, the last blanket ripped and flew into the night, down to the ground where the eaters lay.

"Oh Kelly, it came off!" She looked up at me. "You'll have to jump a bit." Her body shook with cold, and I think a bit of worry too. She wasn't sure I could.

I can. My feet felt the absence of fabric. I was on the last one. I held on tight and I swung. The night was silent. I saw the dead creatures down below, red running into the snow. I saw the nervous teenager wringing her hands. But I saw nothing to fear. I knew I could let go and jump. I can. And do you know why?

Because I have guts.

Little Sister

"Sylvia, wait." Jessica dug her sneakers into the loose gravel. She pulled on Sylvia Plath's pink leash. The pug gave an indignant snort.

"I know, I know." She looked down at the wrinkled, fawn dog and then back up at the dead end. The gravel path they were currently on now gave way to a steep incline of rotted stumps and scratchy leaves. But there were three unmarked dirt paths snaking into the woods before them. They all looked the same, three identical doors back into the deep forest.

There was a chance, Jessica supposed, that all three of them could lead back to the main entrance of the nature preserve. There was also the chance, she knew very well, that none of them did, and that she and Sylvia could spend the entire rest of the day making even more pointless circles in the brush.

"Okay, I bet you're thirsty girl." Jessica let Sylvia lead her down a small ravine to a shallow creek. Sylvia plunged her flat face into the stream and happily lapped up the grimy water, her twisted cinnamon bun tail wagging eagerly.

While she drank, Jessica kept a hold of Sylvia's leash tightly, watching carefully for another human to emerge on the gravel path. Oh, how she would love to see another person, a couple holding hands, or even a group of Boy Scouts looking for a campsite. She could ask for directions then, or even use someone's cell phone and bring up Google fucking maps. How unorganized and stupid she had been.

Jessica strained to think of a good memory. She remembered an autumn afternoon, the perfect sort of day. It had been a bit cool, but the sun still warmed her cheeks.

Her father had taken Jessica, then about eight years old, and her older sister, Tina, to the Olmsted County Fair. After feasting on caramel apples and petting some goats, they had entered the corn maze. The gaping entrance, decorated with plastic skeletons and rusty pitchforks, scared Jessica. But their dad had been so strong and sure as they fought through the dry stalks of corn. The girls followed him and soon Jessica was comforted by his confidence. Even when they came to a dead end, he would just laugh and turn around. When they found the exit, a large curve cut into the high corn and lined with hay bales, her father acted as though he knew it was there all along.

Jessica wished her father was here to guide her through this mess now. His slow, precise way of talking would soothe her mind. He wouldn't let her think bad thoughts. He never did. When the darkness threatened her brain he would always seem to arrive in time, her savior in flannel and dusty work boots. Just the image of him now; tall and muscled, picking at the rough skin around his fingernails, calmed the panicked voice blaring in her head. She tried to think only of her dad as Sylvia got her fill of the creek. But the other thoughts, virulent and mean, flooded inside.

She didn't want to admit to herself it had been hours of loops and backtracking with useless Sylvia tugging in front as though she knew the way. Unlike that day thirty years ago in the corn maze, it was not refreshing autumn, but rather deep into summer and Jessica could feel her grey Henley and khakis sticking to her flesh. Her long blonde hair was particularly sticky, and of course poor Sylvia was not built for such heat. She often stopped to catch her breath, her tongue swollen and bobbing in the air.

Jessica and Sylvia climbed up out of the ravine. They stopped before the three dirt paths.

"We're lost," she said to the dog.

It was the first time Jessica allowed the idea to soak into her consciousness. The word "lost" came with a siege of images. She imagined her abandoned Jeep in the parking lot, weeds growing into the hood. There was her cell phone, bright yellow and useless, in the middle console just waiting to be bagged as evidence by the police.

Jessica thought of her Literature and Society students ready with books and laptops, waiting for a teacher that would never come. There was an image of her ex, Mike, a professor of chemistry with old fashioned corduroy patches on his sleeves and a weak, floppy moustache. He wouldn't even notice Jessica was missing; he had receded back into the shadows as soon as her older sister had meddled in their life.

The last horrific portrait was of skeletons, a young woman and a pug in the tall grass, dead and forgotten. She felt she must be trapped in a bad dream, the sort of nightmare you wake from with a rush of relief. But then Sylvia punctuated the silence with another snort and Jessica knew she most certainly was awake. They both were. Shaking with the realization, Jessica chose the dirt path in the middle. It looked the most used, the most developed. It looked like it led back to humanity.

"It's Tina's fault," Jessica said, as she pushed past an overgrown prickly bush. She was now grateful for choosing long sleeves.

It was difficult to speak through the heat and the fear, but Jessica felt a certain need to share. "Tina thinks..." She stopped to bend down and retie her floppy shoelaces. "She thinks she can say whatever she wants, you know? And that it doesn't matter that I, or anyone really, have feelings." She was aware only Sylvia could hear her, but Jessica liked the cathartic nature of talking to the panting, sniffling creature next to her. Besides, at this rate she may be living in the woods alone with Sylvia forever. They had to start sharing their feelings.

As though to illustrate this exact point, the dog stopped and gave a whine. Jessica waited as Sylvia crouched and peed aside a rotting tree stump. She then began to circle the stump and sniff. Jessica wondered if other dogs had been here, if Sylvia could smell their essence. That idea made her feel better; perhaps they hadn't wandered off the reserve after all.

As Sylvia forced her flat nose deeper into the roots, something large rustled behind a collection of oak trees about twenty feet up the dirt trail. Jessica sucked in her breath and listened. She had the oddest thought shoot through her. She believed, for just a split second, that her father would walk out from the trees, his long arms wide open for a hug. He would whisper that everything was okay into her ear and the panic would lessen, the fear would subside and she wouldn't be lost anymore. But the green leaves trembled and then suddenly stopped. Then they shook again with great effort, as though something was trying to pull them from the bark. Sylvia stiffened and began to pull the leash taut, a low grumble bubbled in her throat. Jessica saw a swish of something moving impossibly fast, something golden yellow.

Curly blonde hair.

The figure was barely a shadow. It was more of an outline than an actual thing. It was shaky but quick, and it moved behind another cluster of trees before Jessica could get a full picture.

She had seen the blonde curls though. Of that she was sure.

The hazy outline quivered in the foliage. It emitted an electric hum that made her think instantly of the steady, low vibrations of a window air conditioner. Growling Sylvia used all of her strength to tug Jessica toward the strange thing behind the leaves, but Jessica stood still, her hands red and straining around the leash.

"Hell…hello?" Jessica heard a scared voice, shaking and dry. She realized it was her own, yet it sounded unattached, far away from her own body.

The shadow and its electric whine evaporated into the humid air.

They were alone again. Jessica could actually sense Sylvia's muscles relaxing. The leash began to slacken in her tight fist. The pug seemed to forget about the enemy and began to absently lick at her paw. But Jessica felt a vulnerable terror. She shuddered violently. Her body shook and twitched until she concentrated on steadying her breath.

"One hippopotamus…, two hippopotamus…., three hippopotamus…," Jessica continued in a calm voice until she reached fifty. She counted slow and methodical just like her father had trained her to do. She could picture him now, just as he had been on the night of her sophomore sweetheart dance.

He sat with her on the back porch, his ratty robe too short for his hairy legs. She cried so hard it felt as though something had come dislodged from her chest. She beat the porch rails with her newly manicured nails, coral pink, and sobbed into her father's chest. That was the night she had known Tina would never let her be happy. Her big sister was both mean and pretty, the most vicious of combinations, and she harbored none of the anxiety and dread that plagued the eternally plump and awkward Jessica.

"Relax, Jessie. Just count it away," her father said that night, that night that had begun with so much promise, but quickly devolved into her realizing Foster Ammon had no interest in Jessica, his eager date, but had orchestrated a plan to date her older sister, Tina. Her father held her hands down and counted along with her as she shook violently from the rage and the understanding. She wished she could feel the pressure of his hands on her now.

Now, Jessica tried, rather clumsily, to soothe herself. To tell herself that what she had seen and heard was just a product of the heat. It was probably an animal, a harmless squirrel searching for acorns, and her mind had created a monster. Sylvia had been anxious though, she hadn't liked the thing with the tight pin curls.

Once Jessica could feel her legs and exhale without shaking, she took a step forward. They continued into the dense woods.

As they got deeper, the thickening canopy of trees blocked the sun. Jessica felt less sticky and Sylvia breathed easier through her squashed nose.

"It's getting late. Don't you think, Sylvia?"

Jessica knew the drop in temperature wasn't only because of the thick trees. The sun was making its final descent and soon it would be dark. Her stomach gave a lurch and she was oddly made aware of how hungry and thirsty she was for the first time. She had been at the reserve since before sunrise and she hadn't consumed a thing. The ache in her stomach was nothing though compared to the horror shaking her entire body. Her panic gave way to nervous giggles thinking of her protector, little Sylvia Plath, tearing the limbs off of a fearsome bear.

Perhaps Tina had been right. Jessica needed a protector. A big hulking dog with a set of razor teeth and angry eyes. Of course when Tina suggested a dog for protection it was just her subtle way to imply Jessica was going to be alone forever. No man was going to stand before a stranger and protect Jessica, so she might as well get a pit bull.

Tina had made sure of this for the entirety of their lives. She had effortlessly taken Foster and discarded him a few weeks later, when Jessica's heart was still a throbbing, open wound. And Foster, the punk rock skateboarder with a surprisingly earnest smile, was only the first. As they grew older Tina didn't bother with stealing men anymore. She would just pick at them in her superior, haughty way until they faded away, leaving Jessica alone, always alone. She thought of Tina then as she always was, sitting at her kitchen table, smoking an endless string of cigarettes and being a sanctimonious bitch. Jessica felt rage. But she didn't try to escape the feeling; she lingered in it because it was much more comforting, and familiar, then the fear.

Jessica and Sylvia walked on. They hadn't seen another human or even another dog since dawn, before she got all agitated and unorganized.

Jessica was comforted by the small woodland animals skittering beside them in the brush. The birds and foxes reminded her that the world was still going on as it should be. They didn't scare her because she instantly could recognize their animalistic movements. Unlike the scary figure, the little animals moved in a predictable pattern. Perhaps most importantly, they interested Sylvia but did not elicit her full on pug attack mode. More than that, Jessica had been in the silence of the woods so long she worried everything had crumbled away and instead of a single day, she and Sylvia had been missing for decades. The creatures seemed to make it all real. Life was still chugging along. Sylvia's snuffles helped Jessica feel grounded too. All she had to do was look at Sylvia's impossibly squished face to feel a tinge of comfort.

"We're going to drive to Leslie's after this, Sylvia. I promise you. We're going to get two milkshakes, one for each of us. And we're going to have the double burgers. You can even have cheese on yours. And we're going to get the twisty fries, the ones that are a little spicy, but not too spicy. Oh and I'm getting a huge Coke with extra ice. I'm going to fill it up at least three times."

Sylvia walked on, anxious, Jessica imagined, to get to Leslie's. Jessica tried to concentrate on their prize too, on the ice cold Coke, but it was getting darker. She stopped suddenly, hoping to hear the sound of a mountain biker whizzing past the tall grass, or the start of an engine or just a human voice. Nothing. Just the sound of Sylvia's panting and Jessica's own heart thumping in her chest. This was bad, and it was going to continue to get worse. Jessica knew there would be no Leslie's tonight, or maybe, ever.

The path led them to a small clearing. Jessica found a soft patch of grass and fell down onto her back, exhausted. Sylvia snuggled into her armpit, thankful for the rest. Hot tears gushed from Jessica's eyes. She was surprised by the overwhelming emotion. She worked so hard to keep it inside, as her dad had taught her, to sit on things and not let the world see her anger, her worry, her panic. But there seemed to be no world now, just a past and no future. She was trapped in a bizarre nothing, a purgatory shared with a clueless pug. Worried, Sylvia pressed her cold nose into Jessica's neck. Jessica hugged her in return. She was grateful to not be completely alone.

"It's going to be okay," Jessica said through the snot and tears running down her lips. "Even if we have to sleep on the ground we'll be okay." She ran her fingers through Sylvia's short, tan coat. A puff of fur settled in her hand. Tina always complained that the dog shed at an irritating rate.

"The couch is covered!" Tina would screech. "Covered!"

Jessica pressed her eyelids closed until she could see faint, sparkling stars in the inner darkness. Tina had done this. Her sister had pushed her to be confused, then made her to lose her step, and, now, end up here, lost. And the worst part of this whole, horrible situation was that Jessica could picture Tina's face, red-cheeked and smiling, because she was right. Jessica really was as useless as Tina had predicted. Early that morning she went into a park, a collection of trails made for leisure and the appreciation of nature, and she vanished like a child. Somehow Jessica had crossed into the deep woods of Minnesota with a pug on a bright, pink leash and she was going to die here. Tina would laugh. She always laughed.

~

Jessica woke to the sensation of her chin shivering so hard her teeth clacked together. She had fallen asleep in a fetal position, wrapped around Sylvia. She twisted her head up and looked at the darkening sky. Her entire body was drenched in a strange, icy sweat that made the summer twilight feel more like a winter. She instinctively rubbed her hands on Sylvia's warm fur and pulled the dog closer to her face. The pug remained asleep. In the diminishing light, Jessica looked down at her companion's scrunched face and smiled. Without Sylvia she would be so much worse off, so alone.

Jessica's body ached from her unexpected nap on the grass. Although she had the urge to stretch her legs and wiggle her toes awake, she stayed still. She didn't want to wake Sylvia from her deep sleep. For the first time that day, Jessica noticed how dirty her hands were. She could barely see her fingers, as night was coming fast, but she could make out the dirt compacted under her nails. She studied each nail and tried to pick out some of the blackness. This made her think of her father again, of his habit of picking at his cuticles. But this also made her think dark thoughts. She had a memory of digging under a similarly dark sky. Of her long, uneven nails digging into the moist soil, and of Sylvia, sitting patiently beside her, but whining softly.

Jessica pushed the exhausting memory into the locked chest inside her mind. Yet another coping device her father had employed her with. She rested her head on Sylvia's body and took in the dog's comforting scent.

"It's going to be okay," Jessica whispered in the dark. "Tomorrow will be better." Her fragmented thoughts led back to her sister again. Tina walked these trails every morning and could surely navigate her way out.

Jessica was surprised to feel herself actually missing Tina. Yes, she would surely make fun of her, but even so, Jessica craved for her big sister to be beside her. They wouldn't be in this mess. Instead they really would be at Leslie's eating their double burgers and laughing about it all.

There was a loud, pulsating hum in the black air. Jessica knew it wasn't a sound made by an animal, or even another human. She knew the figure from before had come back and was close, very close.

She shot up on to her feet as though she had been charged with the same electricity and stared into the blackness. Sylvia slept deeply, unaware of any presence in the night.

"Please. Please leave us alone. We're lost and scared and we won't hurt you. We don't want to hurt anyone."

Jessica could only see the far off stars and the glowing, crescent moon. She was aware of the tall, ancient trees lining the small clearing. But much like the figure, they were only vague outlines now. It could be anywhere, so she spun on her heels in a circle, desperate to see it.

Then the hair came into view. It was up high. God, it was in a tree, perched on a branch like an owl. Its curls glowed like a golden fire. Jessica looked up, her mouth twisting and opening in a silent scream. The figure formed into something human. It still vibrated and pulsed, but now it was a girl. The girl with the fire curls wore a pink gingham dress. She was about ten and she wore the happy grin of a carefree child. She rested her back against the trunk and was somehow held up by the skinny, crackling branches. A caramel apple, affixed to a stick, appeared in the girl's tiny fingers. She began to lick it.

Jessica heard the girl's teeth crunch into the hard caramel coating. The surreal snap made Jessica fall onto her back. The girl carried on, smacking and slurping on her treat. She didn't seem to notice Jessica scooting away on the ground beneath her.

"Tina?" Jessica flailed in the grass. She was on her ass, still looking up at the thing that was sort of a girl. But her arms were furiously pushing her backward. Her palms dug in behind her and she used her feet to help her trajectory. All she cared about was distancing herself from the specter in the tree. Jessica knew her jelly legs couldn't run. She was dimly aware of Sylvia curled up in the grass, oblivious to the horror.

"Tina, please, I don't understand," she managed a strangled whisper. The thing that looked like ten year old Tina Martin didn't look down at her, and for this Jessica was grateful. She thought if she looked into Tina's emerald eyes she would fall into them and never climb back out. She was sure of this more than she was sure the Tina in the tree was real.

Jessica had a flash of memory, a bubbling up from the poorly locked chest in her mind, as she continued to push her limp, scared body backward through the grass. She remembered emerald green, imploring eyes searching her face, trying to find something, humanity perhaps or just a glimpse of familiarity.

Then it was dark, inky and complete. There were no fire curls in the tree. There was no caramel apple, no pink gingham. Jessica was alone, her back now pushed up against what felt like a tree trunk. She couldn't see Sylvia, but was relaxed by the sound of the dog's deep, guttural snores. Jessica remembered her calming exercises. She counted in rhythm with the pug's snotty exhales.

The next sensation was warmth. The sun was already blazing and Jessica instantly felt the sweat between her thighs. Her eyes burned from the assault, so she buried her face into Sylvia's ample belly. She must have crawled her way back to the dog sometime in the night, but she couldn't remember. Or perhaps, she thought, Sylvia had sought her out and nestled against her. It hardly mattered.

Sylvia whined. She was probably thirsty. Jessica's throat was a desert, so surely Sylvia's was too.

"I know girl, I know." Jessica sat up and put an arm over her eyes. She would have to slowly adjust to the blinding sun. She felt Sylvia's curly tail thump against her body. This indicated to Jessica instantly that someone was nearby, someone was on the trail. She peeked over her shoulder.

There was a man. And beside him was a boy, no more than twelve. They both wore bike helmets, but Jessica couldn't see their bikes. The boy held a butterfly net against his chest with an awkwardly skinny arm. The sunlight reflected off his glasses in a sharp burst. They were staring at her with squinted eyes and identical pressed lines for mouths.

"Oh my god, oh thank god." Jessica jumped up onto her unsteady feet. "Please I'm lost." She looked down at the pug, "we're lost."

"Jesus Christ lady. Are you alright?" The man took a hesitant step off the dirt and into the grass.

Jessica nodded. "Yes, we just need some water we're so thirsty, and directions back to my car. I parked at the main entrance of the reserve, but we got all turned around."

He stared at Jessica and Sylvia. A frown pulled down his already serious face. "You're covered."

"Hmm?" Jessica didn't understand.

"You're covered, I mean..."

"You got blood all over ya," the boy said.

She looked down at her long sleeve Henley and khaki pants, her usual professor clothes. But her grey sleeves were mottled with dark, red patches. The red was dry, but she could smell a faint iron scent. There were explosions of crimson on her pants. They looked like blood fireworks.

"It's in your hair." The man's voice trembled. "Are you hurt?"

"Oh no, no!" Jessica laughed. Raising a tentative hand to her head, she realized it seemed awfully gummy.

The boy grabbed at his dad's arm with both hands, letting the large, white net fall to his feet. "Dad?" The man stepped backward and stood in front of the boy.

Jessica found it odd. The way he moved, it was like he was scared of her, or perhaps it was Sylvia.

"She won't bite you. She's real good. I named her Sylvia Plath. Her name was Tuffy before that. Can you believe that? Tuffy!" Jessica giggled.

Sylvia snorted.

"Oh and this, don't worry, it's not mine. It's blood, but I'm not hurt. It's Tina's blood," she confessed. It felt good to talk to a person. To open the chest up a bit. "She walks her dog out here every morning and you know she has never gotten lost. She never gets lost or scared. She gets mad though. At me."

She thought of her sister's face when she unexpectedly met her on the trail. Tina had been real mad then, her nose flared and her hands tightened into fists. Jessica figured her big sister must have known why she was there. Tina had chased Mike away, all of them away, offering her opinions on Jessica's problems and picking, picking. When Tina saw the knife, large and glinting in the morning light, fear had permeated the final moments of her life. That had confused Jessica, that had made her unorganized and forgetful. It had almost made her feel bad, as she buried Tina, to remember her like that, different and not her usual bitchy self.

"And at Tuffy, she gets mad at Tuffy all the time and yells at her, " Jessica continued. She sensed something strange on the man's face. It was as though he didn't understand. "No, it's okay, because I have Sylvia and I love her. I don't care if she snores or sheds on my rug. And now we're going to go to Leslie's and we're going to get milkshakes. It's okay because we have each other. I can talk to her."

Jessica looked down at her big sister's dog and smiled.

Underneath

Twenty-one-year-old Dana Franklin scooped the last shards of butterscotch caramel swirl and smushed it into the waffle cone.

"Anything else tonight?" She handed the elderly couple a pair of napkins with their ice cream.

"That'll do." The man wearing a sweatshirt declaring he was indeed The Best Papa in the Universe gave Dana a ten dollar bill. "Keep the change," he hollered over his shoulder as he followed his wrinkled wife out into the spring evening.

Dana, quite familiar with the prices, knew her tip would amount to about four cents. She frowned.

The parking lot of Pistol Pete's Ice Cream and Fudge Shoppe was empty now, aside from Dana's Honda Civic, a greyish pinkish car with a neon rope holding the back bumper on. The sun was dipping below the mountains, which meant her shift would be over soon. It was May, before Memorial Day, so Dana had a few more weeks of getting home early before the summer rush forced her to scoop ice cream until eleven at night.

She was alone. She felt a pull to take a bathroom break.

Pistol Pete's was at the end of a dead end road, past the Gold Mine Mini-Golf Course and tucked into the side of the forest. She couldn't hear any vehicles sputtering down Prospector Street, so she figured she had time.

Her cell said it was 6:51. In a little over an hour, she would be at her apartment, curled up under Princess Leia, her yellow lab, watching TV.

Dana went into the bathroom, a unisex room with just one toilet, and locked the door. She went straight for the mirror hung above the dripping sink. Her face was a roadmap of scars. There were dozens of marks, across her forehead, down her cheeks, under her nose and lining her lips. Some of them were a deep, irritated red. Others were scabbing over and a few were nearly healed. Dana noticed a pimple on her cheekbone, it pulsed under her skin, begging for release. She ran a finger over it, already feeling relief, already feeling the tightness in her chest lessen.

She didn't see her chestnut hair lining her oval face or her sparkling green eyes in her reflection. She could see only varying degrees of necessity, bumps, pimples and rough patches that needed her.

But first she raised up her shirt, dull white with ice cream stained long sleeves, to inspect her belly. Her flat stomach was red and swollen from right underneath her A-cup bra down to where her khakis made a patterned indent into her waist. There were pin marks, familiar and soothing to Dana, surrounding each scab and bump.

She didn't bring her pin to work, in fact it never left her bathroom at home, so she would have to rely on her fingernails.

Nothing on her stomach demanded immediate attention so Dana smoothed her shirt down. She leaned over the sink, as close to the mirror as she could manage with her feet still on the ground. She zeroed in on the blemish, calling for her, needing her. The dripping of the faucet and the loud hum of the commercial ice cream freezers left her ears. She could see and hear only her fingernails, ragged and covered in cracking, magenta polish, squeezing her skin. The pressure was glorious, exultant, everything.

The ultimate satisfaction would be a white pus. Something juicy and even, God, even a popping sound. That would make her shudder with happiness.

But the squeeze would have to do.

Dana watched a clear sort of liquid ooze out of the inflamed zit and then finally blood began to drip down her face.

There was a part of her, deep down and often with the voice of a child, which urged her to stop. Yet she pressed on, her fingers feeling numb, her right eye twitching with the pain. She could feel the weight of her focus on her cheekbone, hot and searing.

She was vaguely aware of the blood, now dangling at the end of her jaw, threatening to fall on the faucet.

A sound, too loud to ignore, rattled out in the shop and into the bathroom. Dana had the instinct to look, to turn her head, but she just needed to squeeze a bit longer, just a few seconds more.

It was a customer surely, a group perhaps with raucous children swinging from the ice cream counter.

Dana swallowed hard. She would have to settle for unfinished. Her skin was an incomplete project. Even after hours of poking and picking she felt she had missed the finish line.

She took a single square of toilet paper and pressed it on her pimple. Blood soaked through the white. She splashed a handful of cold water on her face.

Her cheek pulsed with pain. But more than that, it pulsed with anger of its imperfect treatment. She would have to use her pin later.

"I'm so sorry to keep you waiting," Dana announced as she swung the bathroom door open and entered the shop. "What can I get…" She stopped. Her hand, reaching out for a pair of scooping gloves, lingered in the air.

A woman, in a full, puffy bridal gown pushed a mint green chair against the front doors of Pistol Pete's. Her silky black hair swung with the effort.

Dana watched as the woman leaned over the chair and inspected the deadbolt.

"Is this all? Do you have a chain?" The bride looked over her bare shoulder. Her dress was strapless, with a dozen white buttons trailing down the back. She was Asian, with a porcelain complexion and long black eyelashes.

Dana nodded dumbly.

"Well get it!" The bride screeched. The woman retrieved another chair, this one buttercream yellow, from one of the few tables and scraped it against the floor. She placed it against the glass door, panting. Dana retrieved the chain, used for locking up after closing, from the back room. She felt she had entered a strange dream somehow, confusing and nonsensical.

"Put it on! Put it on!" The gown swished underneath the beautiful woman as she paced the shop.

"On the outside or the inside?" Dana held the cold metal links in her hands.

"Inside! Don't open the door!"

Dana obeyed. She applied the chain to both door handles as the manager had taught her, only now on the inside for the first time. Her hands shook as she clicked the padlock. The bride couldn't stop moving. She rushed from window to window.

"The tables are bolted down?"

"Yeah." Dana felt for the padlock key in her pocket. She wanted to be sure it was there. She rubbed her fingers over the familiar shape.

The bride pushed one more chair against the glass. Dana noticed the woman's arm was bleeding, spattering the front of her white gown with a fine mist of red.

"You're bleeding." Dana pointed to the woman's wrist. There was so much of it, dripping down her arm and even on the floor. Dana felt faint. She could handle her own blood, pricked with her own nails, but that was different. She slumped down into one of the chairs.

"Yep. I am." The woman continued to flit around the shop, looking for furniture. "Are there more doors?" Her eyes scanned everywhere.

Dana forced herself to look away from the gory wrist. She settled on staring at the ceiling. "There's a back entrance. It's locked."

She heard the bridal dress swish around the woman's legs as she ran to check the back door.

"Come help me! Hey! Come here!" The bride called.

Dana hesitated. Her pimple was throbbing more than ever. But the sounds of the woman's ragged breaths finally compelled Dana to stand. She walked slowly to the back room, afraid of what has happening, what she would find.

The bride was trying to push a large freezer. She was petite and her injured arm was clearly bothering her. She had smeared some blood on the top of the appliance. Her black hair hung around her face as she pushed. "Please help me." Her shrill yell had become a pleading whisper.

Dana bent down and unplugged the freezer. She had an instant flash of her pug-faced manager, Darren, who would surely faint at the sight of an unplugged freezer filled with ice cream. But, Dana was becoming increasingly sure she was inside her own dream. Perhaps she had squeezed too hard and she had fainted onto the grimy bathroom tile. Or maybe she had finally succumbed to the boredom of the day and nodded off behind the ice cream counter. She was probably drooling into a collection of ice cream scoops while having this bizarre nightmare.

She got on her knees and used both hands to press down the clamps holding each of the four wheels. Her movements felt slow, underwater, as though she were watching herself remotely. She stood up and began to push the freezer in front of the door. She knew that's where it was going. They were clearly keeping something out.

The bride pushed weakly; her adrenaline clearly dropping. Thankfully, the wheels made it pretty easy to get the heavy freezer in front of the back entrance.

"Thank you," The woman whispered, wrapping her left hand around her injured wrist. Blood squeezed through her small fingers. A large diamond ring, square cut and surrounded by smaller diamonds, sparkled in the dim, back room light.

"Um…" Dana didn't know what to say.

The two women walked back to the front of the shop.

"We have a first aid kit, under the counter," Dana offered.

The bride didn't seem to hear. Instead she stood with her head bent to the side, watching the setting sun as it created mysterious pink shadows atop the mountains.

"We had such nice weather today. Everyone kept saying we should prepare for rain in early May. My mom said we should've waited until June actually."

Dana, unsure of what to do with her body, stood behind the ice cream counter.

"It was a pretty day," she added, picking up a wash rag and folded it, concentrating on the feel of the fabric and lining the edges perfectly.

Her face was hot with need. Her pimple was ready now, swollen and volcanic. That sensation, a familiar torture, made her think it wasn't a dream after all.

But the bride, in her pure, fluffy white dress, and her raven hair and her dramatic red lips looked unreal, fantastical.

"My name is Jennifer." The bride didn't move from her post at the large front window. She rested her injured wrist on the glass.

"I'm Dana."

"Do you hear that?"

Dana shook her head.

"It's the police and fire department, probably ambulances too. Although…" Jennifer trailed off.

They stood, silently. Dana stared at the empty container of butterscotch caramel swirl. Its replacement was currently melting in the back room. If this was real, if she was living this, Darren would fire her and she would lose her apartment and her life and even Princess Leia. She couldn't be homeless again.

"What's going on?" Dana finally asked. Her anxiety churned on full blast. She wanted her pin, she wanted a mirror.

Jennifer lingered at the window.

"You're bleeding. We should wrap it up," Dana said. "You're getting it all over your dress."

The bride snorted. She turned, her red lips twisted in an ironic smile. "I wouldn't worry about my dress, Dana. Besides, you're bleeding too."

Dana immediately slapped her hand to her cheek. A bit of red smudged into her fingers. She had overdone this one. She should know better at work. She should have focused on a bump on her belly, or her thigh. Darren had made it clear people didn't want to see bleeding scars dripping over their ice cream cones.

"You shouldn't pick at your zits, it makes it worse," Jennifer said, flitting behind the counter. For the first time Dana could see a brown ring of dirt on the bottom of her wedding dress. Jennifer's bare feet poked out, well-manicured but dirty. Dana wondered where the bride's presumably expensive shoes were now. In a pile in the woods? Strewn on the lawn of the resort?

"Should we call someone? The police?" Dana kept her hand on her cheek.

Jennifer nodded. "I'm sure they're all at the lodge by now, but I guess you should tell them we're alive over here."

There was something ghostlike about Jennifer's movements and expressions. She seemed not to blink.

Dana realized the bride was in shock. Her face was pale and her dark eyes couldn't seem to focus on anything at all.

Dana dropped her hand and pulled out her cell phone. Now she could hear a distant siren, up by the lodge as Jennifer had said. She punched in the numbers 911 and shakily raised the phone to her ear.

She was preparing her speech for the operator, a bizarre description of the last twenty minutes of her life. But there was no answer. She finally checked to make sure she had pressed the correct number.

"They won't pick up." Dana felt she was underwater again, in slow motion. Her pimple throbbed.

Jennifer continued to stare forward. Her mouth slackened and her eyes blazed with fear. She looked past the shelf holding a collection of homemade fudge into what Dana supposed could only be an unknown, terrifying memory.

"Jennifer?" Dana waved her cell phone. "Jennifer, they won't pick up."

Jennifer gave a weak nod.

Fear for her life, more powerful than her needling anxiety, more powerful than her worry of losing her job, pounded through Dana's heart.

She ended her phone call and set her cell aside.

Dana surveyed her workplace. Pistol Pete, a cartoon prospector with an enormous white moustache looked down at her from his post above the glass doors. He held a sack tied with a ratty rope thrown over his bony shoulder, marked with a big gold dollar sign, and in the other fist he held an impossibly high ice cream cone, twelve scoops high. His usual eager smile had somehow turned into a disapproving sneer in the waning evening light. Dana looked away from his watchful eyes.

The pastel chairs, usually bright and cheery, looked oddly joyless in a pile against the door. The long, low counter with the glass hood protecting the ice cream from snot and sticky children's hands was tomblike now, a useless, silent stretch of nothing.

"Who's out there? Who are we hiding from?" Dana stepped around the counter and toward the small bride.

Jennifer finally looked up at Dana. A fake eyelash fluttered down her perfect cheek. "Do you believe we can really know people? Like…do you think you can know someone fully?"

Dana rubbed her hands on her thighs. She formed an image in her mind, of Jennifer producing a large knife from under her dress. One covered in blood and hidden in the white folds. Perhaps it was this delicate woman she needed to be afraid of.

"Tell me! Tell me! Who wants to hurt you? " Dana was surprised by how her own weak voice transformed into something almost powerful.

"Oh my." Jennifer looked at her red and gummy wrist. "I don't think we're safe in here. Do you have more chains?"

Dana simmered. She was choking on her fear now, it enveloped her entire body. She had to get some sort of answer before she burst.

"Jennifer," she lowered her voice, trying to rein in the new anger that had surged in with the fear. She felt as though she were speaking to a distracted child. "I need you to please, please tell me what is scaring you? Why are you here? Where are the police?"

"They're at the lodge."

"Yes, okay. Now what happened at the lodge?"

Jennifer squeezed both fists. "I think I need to go back. I need to go back and find Stephen."

Dana wanted to slap her. She wanted to slap her so hard a red handprint would appear on her flawless skin.

"Is Stephen your husband?" Dana trembled.

"My fiancé. Oh. Oh I guess he is my husband now."

Dana took another step forward. She placed her hand on Jennifer's bare shoulder. Her skin felt clammy. "Is there someone out there with a gun? Did someone hurt you?"

"No, no, no." The bride dipped her shoulder to get away from Dana's touch. "No gun."

Dana drew her hand back and looked out the glass front. The sun was now just a razor thin orange line. Dark swallowed her Honda.

"We're going to get in my car and drive toward the sirens. Okay?" Dana said.

She looked forward to the moment she could pass over the shocked and morose bride to a police officer. She looked forward to coming back and cleaning the store before Darren arrived the next morning, hungover and incredibly cranky like every day. She looked forward to watching the local news, an ice cold Miller Lite resting on her burning belly, to get some sort of clue about what was going on. She looked forward to her bathroom mirror and her pin.

Jennifer agreed to get in the car. Her little body was beginning to shake all over, but her rounded jaw jutted out with determination.

Dana pushed the parlor chairs away from the door and released the chain. She walked out into the spring evening first, twisting her head from side to side to make sure Leatherface himself wasn't waiting atop his rusted pickup, whirring chainsaw in hand.

There was nothing but a pleasant evening breeze. Dana flinched when an empty, cardboard ice cream cup skittered across the pavement toward her. A bright pink spoon rolled behind.

Slobs. Use a trashcan. Yet her skin was covered in goosebumps from the windblown trash.

Jennifer placed a tentative foot outside. She held the sides of her white dress, blood now drying into a sticky jam on her wound. She wiggled her toes to sense the air. The sight of it all made Dana reach for her pimple. She felt the sore skin and pressed in hard with her finger, to feel more.

They climbed into the Honda. The distant buzz of sirens continued, which Dana found rather comforting.

She started the engine.

Jennifer struggled to get the belt over her gown. The tulle was everywhere, spread on the dash, stuffed in the console.

"Fuck it." She finally let the seatbelt snap back.

"Do you mind?" Dana pointed to a pack of cigarettes hiding in a hole of cords that had once held a CD player. "I'll roll down the windows."

Jennifer shrugged. She looked down at her own small hands, the hefty diamond ring now ruddy with crusted blood. "Can I have one too?"

Dana handed her one and slipped another into her mouth. She fished out her lighter, bright pink, and lit them both.

Jennifer doubled over from coughing. She held her simmering cigarette as she spat into her white, lacy lap. Dana cranked down her window, as though it might help.

"Ah…sorry…"she hacked. "I haven't had one of these since college."

Dana smiled. She imagined Jennifer was a good girl. She probably had a sensible career and a clean house with a vegetable garden and probably a treadmill she actually used. Or maybe she went to the gym, with an organized bag slung over her tiny shoulder. She probably went with Stephen and they ran laps together.

Jennifer swallowed her cough.

They began to drive down the winding road, down the mountain.

Dana tried to look straight ahead. There were no cars parked at the mini golf lot, too late for early spring, but the Old West Buffett had a collection of cars. Some people, nosy old ones, were out on the wrap around porch, looking up toward the lodge, wondering about the sirens. They watched Dana's car with interest.

For a moment Dana thought of stopping at the buffet. She could swing in and get some help. But she wasn't exactly sure she needed help.

Jennifer took a long, deliberate drag from her cigarette. She inhaled the smoke into her lungs and flicked a bit of ash onto her dress.

This unsettled Dana. She pressed her hand into the steering wheel. The need for something sharp rattled in her chest. She pinched her thigh with her other hand.

"Stephen has red hair." Jennifer took another drag. "I've just always liked gingers, the freckles and the whole bit," smoke escaped her lips. "I don't know what's wrong with me." She giggled.

Dana smiled. Her own smoke felt good. The familiar smell was beginning to soak up some of her anxiety.

Jennifer rolled down her own window, once she found the lever underneath the mounds of white material. She tossed the cigarette, smudged with lipstick, out into the night.

Their lodge came into view.

They passed the enormous log pillars on either side of the road signifying they were on the property. Rustic lamps lined the narrowing road.

A siren kept blaring, so loud that Dana could feel the vibrations in her feet.

She drove slowly. A row of cop cars were stopped at various angles on the long drive.

An ambulance was parked near the grand entrance. Its orange flashing lights illuminated the giant willow trees that canopied above them. The back doors stood open. An empty stretcher lay inside.

Dana parked next to the whining ambulance. Her cigarette fell from her mouth, forgotten, as she got out. Fear came again, real and sickening. There were no officers at the front door of the lodge wrapping yellow tape around to keep people away. There were none of those old nosy people, stretching their necks to get a glance of some carnage.

Jennifer exited the Honda. She was an ethereal figure in the night, her dress in perfect contrast to the darkness. Her black hair was beginning to stick to her face, from sweat Dana supposed, but she was still remarkably beautiful.

The small bride considered the empty ambulance.

Dana was about to ask what they should do.

But then Jennifer ran up the concrete steps leading to the main entrance. She held her large dress up with her small hands like a dainty lady about to cross a stream, fearful she may get her petticoats wet. But she moved like a sprinter, her bare feet slapping on the hardness beneath, taking the enormous steps two at a time. Before Dana could comprehend, the bride was gone, through the heavy wood doors and inside the lodge.

Dana's hand instinctively raised up to her cheeks. She felt her blemishes and bumps. She picked at some dry skin on her lip until her eyes watered.

The ambulance kept blaring.

She was going to follow this demented Cinderella into the lodge. She was going to see this through.

Dana jogged up the steps in her sneakers, which made a dull squish on the concrete. She pulled the door open. An eerie silence greeted her in the lobby. There were no employees behind the barn wood front desk.

She couldn't call for Jennifer. It might draw the attention of someone. Some bad person. Also, Dana was sure she was mute from the fear. The bizarreness of the situation poked at her reason, her understanding of the world around her.

So she walked across the tile, the sound of her breath creating an awkward, lonely echo. The hall leading to the ballroom was empty too.

But a smell, iron and all too familiar lingered everywhere.

There was a black shoe sticking out from the ballroom door.

She approached. A million words bubbled within her. Yet she couldn't speak.

The foot was attached to navy blue pants, which were attached to a tucked in navy blue shirt. A shield shaped patch was affixed to his right sleeve with the letters PD standing out in gold stitching. The cop's face was smashed into the floor and he was on his belly, a puddle of dark blood, almost purple, underneath him. His body held the door open. A gun rested under his dead hand.

Dana crouched down and took the pistol. She clutched the cool metal, thankful. She thought about tucking it into the waistband of her khakis but decided on keeping it out, pointed at the room. She maneuvered around the dead cop and entered the ballroom. As she made her way past a table overflowing with cream and white wrapped packages, she realized the entire ballroom was filled with dead bodies.

An older man in a tux, with the same ebony, silky hair as Jennifer was splayed out on top of a table filled with turned over glasses. Champagne dripped on the floor in steady beads.

There was a woman drooping against the wall, with a bloody slash where her neck used to be. She stared at Dana with pale, milky eyes.

There were more, hundreds more, but Dana backed out and carefully climbed over the dead cop before she could really look at them. She would rather remember them as amorphous blobs. As she ran back toward the lobby, gun pointed straight ahead, she could feel the worry bubbling within her. A memory, sharp as a knife, cut through Dana's brain. Her mother had died on the floor. Her mother's eyes had stared forward like that too.

An open patio door, down a wide corridor that led to the gardens, swung in the breeze. Dana nearly shot through the glass panes, but stopped her trembling finger before a bullet could escape. She had a vague notion she would need to save whatever bullets she might have.

She steadied herself, trying to wash the overlapping images of the ballroom and her mother away. Her eyes wanted to close. She wanted to stop for a moment, and maybe even feel the pulse of her pimple. But she couldn't.

Instead she walked through the door. Dana extended her arms in the same V as she had seen cops do on TV. But the gun was heavier than she expected. She willed her wrists to keep it upright.

It was black outside, except for the incessant ambulance lights, that created a stilted, disco ball effect on the lodge's vast gardens.

Dana sipped the fresh air.

But the metal tang of death clung to her as strongly as ice cream had stained her clothes. She would never go back in there. Never.

Another dead policeman was on the ground. It looked as though he had been on the patio and then, as he died, or perhaps right after, he had rolled down the slight hill and into a pile of woodchips dotted with budding yellow tulips.

Dana skidded down the same grassy hill, keenly aware of the body. She kept her distance.

"STEPHEN! STEEEEPHEN!" Jennifer's voice echoed through the night.

Dana saw a swish of white, illuminated in the siren's light. She followed a paved pathway into a hedged maze of flowers. As she smelled how the roses mingled with the bloody scent all around her, she had the distinct realization that she was going to die.

Jennifer paced in front of a babbling fountain. It was a grand modern feature, built with slate rocks and distressed wood.

Dana felt so many words inside of her, fighting to escape. But she could only stare.

"Stephen! You come here! You come here right now!" Jennifer chided.

Dana wondered if Jennifer had seen the ballroom.

She lowered her arms, but continued to grasp the gun with both hands.

The small bride didn't notice Dana. She was looking into the darkness, past the fountain.

Dana strained to see.

"Stephen STOP! You have to STOP!" Jennifer hugged her bare arms. It was getting chilly.

Someone shifted next to the hedge.

Dana took a few steps forward, willing her voice to come back, to announce her presence.

"STEEEPHEN!" Jennifer screeched once more. "PLEASE!"

Stephen emerged from the shadows.

Dana expected a man in a tuxedo, perhaps with a floppy, floral boutonniere tacked to his chest. She expected red, fiery hair and a spatter of freckles across his pale nose.

But Stephen was not a "ginger" as Jennifer had professed.

He had no hair, or nose, for that matter. He was about seven feet tall with two pipe-like, dark green antennae that shimmered oddly in the light of the fountain.

His bulbous insect eyes clicked back and forth. He took a guttural, hitching breath and rubbed his long praying mantis arms together. Each one ended with a curved, sharp claw.

Two crepe thin wings crackled on his back. The enormous insect stepped forward on the paver stones, his reedy limbs red with blood. Jennifer regarded her new husband. Her lips formed an exaggerated 'O' and her chest heaved wildly.

Dana felt hot inside, burning. Her breath caught in her throat and she felt a sudden panic strike her in the stomach.

Stephen, he looked like her mother had, in that final moment when Dana felt the Earth shift and her new reality tear into her body. It was the familiarity of his insect eyes that made Dana's insides seize up.

"It's the face you hide from the mirror Dana, what we hide..." Her mother's words filled the night.

"Stephen....what's happened?" Jennifer covered her mouth with her injured hand. Fat tears rolled down her perfect cheeks.

Stephen opened his ragged looking mandibles to speak. Strange green saliva bubbled out. Dana saw a glimmer of yellow, razor teeth.

Her pimple pounded like a heartbeat. It wanted release. Dana wanted release. But she kept still, she shook her head.

The insect moved quickly, wrapping Jennifer up in his crackling wings. She screamed from inside his embrace. White tulle stuck out the bottom, along with her dirty, bare feet.

Dana was a statue. The gun was slipping from her fingers.

Please. She spoke inside herself.

Please give me the strength. Please. She begged to the same unhelpful God that had allowed her to see her mother's true form. She had been so scared she had pushed her, pushed her and killed her, by accident really, and...

"It's who we are Dana, underneath," her mother said as she had died. But she hadn't spoken with her mouth. Her voice had pierced into Dana's brain, still her mother's voice but somehow alien and threatening. Dana cried, screamed and struggled to understand. Her mother's eyes had been the same, the same eyes from before she had released what was underneath.

I promise. I promise. I promise.

Dana lurched forward, free. "I WON'T...." she clutched the pistol. "I PROMISE I WON'T HURT MYSELF ANYMORE. I promise." The words streamed out like hot, violent vomit. "I PROMISE!" She screamed.

A bullet fired from the gun. It shot through one of the thing's antennae.

Stephen's antennae.

Black tar spilled from the wound.

It, he, reeled back, letting go of Jennifer. The bride fell to the ground, a fresh scratch reddening across her forehead.

The insect shook its head. He spied Dana across the courtyard. His long legs stroked the ground.

Dana thought of the ballroom.

She thought of the cop, falling, ass over tea kettle, down the grassy hill before he could even get his gun from the holster.

Dana accepted her death. It was true then. She could keep her promise and not hurt herself anymore. More than that, she could keep it all in, what was underneath. She could keep it inside.

"RUN!" She yelled to Jennifer.

Time slowed, as she knew it probably would. Stephen flew toward her, five feet off the ground. His limbs rubbed together to create a shrill, unsettling sound that was somehow louder than the never ending siren.

She clicked the trigger but no more bullets came.

Dana closed her eyes and felt peace. Her skin was quiet and content. A breeze from his wings blew her bangs back.

"NOOOOOO!" Jennifer cried. "STEPHEN NOOOO!"

Dana waited for her neck to become a bloody, open slash.

But... But the insect stopped.

He turned toward his bride. He loved her.

Everyone else was in a pile, dead, but Jennifer had only a superficial wound. She was still alive.

"He wants me to go with him," Jennifer said, realization of this truth dawning.

"No." Dana dropped the empty gun.

Jennifer grabbed both sides of her gown and walked toward her Stephen, the real one, the one that had been under the red hair and freckles.

"I want to," Jennifer nodded.

"No."

"He won't hurt anyone else. He just wants me." She managed a crooked smile.

"NO!"

He grabbed Jennifer then, his annoyance of Dana forgotten. His bent, stringy legs encompassed her once more. Her head, so tiny next to his alien, insect frame, stuck out. "He won't hurt you now." She looked comfortable.

The bride and groom flew up, up, toward the silver crescent of the moon. The white dress fluttered in the breeze.

Dana watched him hold her high above the lodge. She thought of an insect nest, sticky and damp. *Please... Please I promise.*

Dana knelt on the hard pavement. Her skin buzzed with need. She could feel the pressure of it, underneath.

Something called her to strip herself away, to remove her skin and meet her true self, the insect inside.

Stephen was weak. He had let the urge overcome him. But Dana didn't grab at her aching cheek. Her itchy hands found a stone, large as a baseball and smooth and cool. She stood.

Jennifer's feet dangled ten feet above her, suspended in the air by her insect groom. Dana had only seconds. She stepped back to see him, somehow shimmering in the night. He was content; he had what he wanted. He didn't expect it. Dana pulled her arm back.

The rock catapulted through the air and hit Stephen's mandible with a surreal SMACK. A screech, far from human, vibrated from his... its chest.

Jennifer slipped immediately. Her dress was caught in the insect's front legs, exposing her bottom half; toned legs with a black lace garter wrapped around one thigh.

Dana jumped up on her tip toes, trying to grab Jennifer's ankle.

The frustrated creature fought to both hold the bride and fly, but its syrupy, black blood poured onto the ground. Dana felt the heat of it on her sneakers.

"JENNIFER!" She tried to grasp her toes. She was just a foot too short.

A gunshot rang out, echoing off the fountain. Dana covered her ears. She turned, again in what felt like slow motion, to see the cop, the one formally face down in the tulips, holding a gun with one hand and his bleeding side with the other.

The thing that was inside a red headed man named Stephen fell to the stoned path in a crumple. Its head resembled a broken egg. Jennifer landed with a soft thud. Her puffy dress protected her. She cried, softly, creating smudgy lines of black mascara down her cheeks.

The cop slipped to the ground, calling for help on the radio strapped to his shoulder.

Dana's knees buckled and she felt the hard stones underneath her. A piercing pain, this one unfamiliar, bloomed inside of her. Her heart hurt. And her skin hurt too. It burned and bubbled and asked for release.

But she realized as her tears washed her clean, she had made a promise.

A promise.

If she kept picking and pulling something would come out. Something she couldn't control. A beast, a monster, a reality that she tried to forget.

She crawled to her new friend, the widow.

Everley

Emily sat in the car with a bag of caramels between her knees. She unwrapped each candy and let the litter fall to the floor while she ate. It was summer and she was the only one in the Everley Nursery School parking lot. Her air-conditioning blasted her face so hard a cold headache had developed, but Emily was not ready to leave. Soon she would pull back down the wooded street and head to Burger King or maybe Taco Bell and pick up her lunch. But for now she would watch the old building until her caramels ran out. This was her truth now, her after life.

She had died with them four years ago. Her parents came and sat with her at her home when Adam and the girls didn't show up. They were missing for hours. The knock came at twilight. Her dad rose from the couch and went to the foyer. Her mom trailed behind, her face white and her hands shaking. The two police officers came in. Emily could hear their steps on the tile as they made their way to her. She would have nightmares years later, nearly every night, of those hesitant steps, the uneasy strides of the grim reaper. Emily wished they hadn't found her door, she wished they hadn't walked into her living room with their matching wide eyes and tight lines for mouths. She wasn't ready to die.

Life continued for other people. But Emily didn't consider what she had a life. She was not living on the same plane of existence as others; she was in a limbo, an uncertain hell that teetered on nothing but blackness.

In her before life she had cared about things like money and keeping her figure. Money had afforded them that last trip to Disney World and the girls went to a nice preschool, the impressive building she sat in front of now, with new swings and fancy art. But in this after life she only bothered to use money for food. She went to the grocery store for junk now, piling buttered popcorn and M&Ms into her basket. She didn't need the big shopping cart with straps anymore.

Emily had heard what her friends said, her mom too, that she was killing herself with fries and grease. They arrived in a group, a mix of her college friends and her fellow playdate moms, offering help. She

71

lived with her parents now, unable to face the empty bedrooms in her own home. They surprised her on a Saturday afternoon, careful not to bring their own children. Her mother sat in the middle of her friends and nodded her head in tacit agreement of the intervention. They wanted to help her, they wanted to pat her hand and hug her and make it okay. She knew they were right but she couldn't care. She was fat, and in her before life she would have hated the idea.

She suspected she weighed more now than when she was nine months pregnant with her twin girls. Her stomach sagged over her sweatpants and her chubby fingers couldn't hold her wedding ring anymore. But all of this didn't matter in her after life. Emily didn't hate herself because there was no self to hate, she was nothing more than a gaping void, a vessel that had once been someone, a ghost.

Everley Nursery School looked the same as it had then. The day, before they had died, Emily had picked the girls up inside its main entrance. While Emily waited, she chatted with Jackson Allen's mom. She was a tall, thin, granola eater with a plump baby girl wrapped in an elaborate cloth carrier strapped to her chest. The following week she came to the funeral with her husband. She had a chalk white face and wet eyes as though her own children had been smashed into the highway. But of course Jackson Allen's mom, and all the other moms, the ones who sent her flowers and made a scrapbook and cooked her a few dinners, they got to go home and live their lives. There was no schism for them. There was no before and after. They had the joy of the linear and the complete.

Emily surprised herself by turning the engine off. Although she often parked at Everley, she hadn't stepped out and felt the ground underneath her since the before time. She swung her door open and let herself find footing on the gravel. The heat that greeted her, that encompassed her entire body like an electric blanket, made her think instantly of summer picnics, the county fair and sex with Adam in the pool.

Emily was emboldened to do something. She just wasn't sure what. As she stepped toward the brick building, there was a welcome breeze that cooled down her already flushed face. Just walking from her car to the cement steps took considerable effort. Her legs shook as she made her way to the front door. She thought about the last time she had turned the handle and pushed.

Now she knew it wouldn't open no matter how hard she pushed. The symmetry of it all seemed right. She tried the door anyway and then cupped her hands and peered into the empty hall. The lights were off and the classroom doors were closed. Emily listened; she pressed her ear to the glass. She didn't hear a janitor or a teacher or anyone. Instead, Emily heard summer sounds, kids shrieking down the street, dogs barking, a far off lawn mower and even the rhythmic pulse of a sprinkler. She stood back and took in the building before her.

Everley had been built at the turn of the nineteenth century as an elementary school for the rich kids of St. Paul. Its gothic beauty had been maintained fastidiously by the board of directors, even after the small class rooms were deemed more appropriate for a nursery school. Aside from the bright and modern playground behind Everley, the grounds and building were distinctly antique. Emily ran her hands over a few of the original bricks. For the first time she really looked at the place, she took in the grand pillars and the thick paned windows. She had always been so busy before, she had her hands full of life. But now in her afterlife she had found herself gazing, staring and gawking at all things.

It wasn't the beauty that she took in; she no longer had the capacity for that. It was rather the permanency of buildings and lakes and rocks which confused her. They had existed before Adam, and Fiona, and Sophie. They still existed. It was such a numbing thought. Everley stood on this summer day, a monument to the joke of life. Emily should be at the cabin with her parents while Adam worked. She should be on the pontoon with the girls and a cooler of pop. She couldn't imagine them being nine now; she could only think of Fiona and Sophie as five and in their matching princess life vests. Life vests.

Emily laughed then, the irony too much to take. The sound, foreign and forgotten, reverberated on the empty concrete and brick surrounding her. She felt a sudden urge to look in the window of the girls' class. It was the one at the very end, behind a considerably large rose bush. She jumped off the porch into the greenery that lined the front of the school. She stopped for a moment, feeling her full weight on her knees and ankles. She felt pain she had never known. It was old, fat people pain she never guessed would be her own. Emily pushed through the lilacs and took a few glances into the other classrooms.

Each window had a thin curtain blocking out the sun, but she could still see inside. There were rugs with the alphabet and bins of toys and play kitchens. There were no formal desks, but rather round tables with tiny plastic chairs for tiny humans. She reached the scratchy rose bush and pushed though anyway, somehow thankful for the prickling pain on her legs. She cupped her hands once more for a good look. She saw the same short tables and little chairs. She wondered which ones Fiona and Sophie had sat in. She was sure they were the same.

Then she saw a boy. He sat in the teacher sized chair, up at the front of the classroom with a book in his lap. He wore jean shorts and she was sure he was about six years old. The book was turned toward the room, toward the others. She hadn't seen them before; she had seen the blue chairs but not them. They were sitting in them, girls and boys.

Emily felt a fear she hadn't known in four long years. Her stomach roiled and turned over. There was something wrong with this scene, with all of them. She watched them watch the boy as they listened to the story. He flipped the pages and pointed to the pictures. She couldn't hear him through the thick glass but she could see his mouth moving on his impossible face. There was something burning inside of her, an alarm, and a panic. She knelt below the window and felt a rock slip into her fingers. It was sharp like the thorns sticking her arms and she liked the weight of it.

Emily stood and pulled her flabby arm back. She began to hit the window with the rock in her fist. She concentrated on her efforts, hitting and punching until she heard the first splitting crack and then the window crumbled into the classroom. Without thinking, she pushed her considerable heft up onto the frame and rolled through the white curtain and onto the floor. As she panted on the hardwood, curled into the fetal position, she was aware of the hot blood trickling down her sides. Her belly had caught some shards on her way through.

The boy was still sitting in the teacher's chair. He held the book open in his bony hands. All of the children's eyes were on her and they were wide and questioning.

Emily sat up. She pressed her back against the wall and held her throbbing stomach. "What are you doing in here? Where are your parents?"

A skinny girl, about thirteen, in a thick plaid dress and long sleeved blouse with a lace collar, jumped up from her tiny chair. Emily watched as her braids swung along with her. The girl walked to the open door that led into the darkened hallway. "I'm going to go get bandages," she announced with a rather snide smirk.

The other children watched the braided girl leave and then they all turned their heads to Emily once again. Emily slumped into the reading nook, exhausted and bleeding. The boy let the book drop from his lap onto the floor as he scooted off the chair and made his way toward her. Emily felt terrified as he kneeled beside her, she couldn't understand why but it was a palpable horror rising in her chest. She wanted to scream.

He had a kind face, but she could read pity in his deep, brown eyes. The hint of pity was something she had grown rather familiar with. Emily studied his smooth cheeks, his thick, dark eyebrows and the slope of his nose. There was something achingly familiar about his outfit, the ragged jean shorts and the faded t-shirt of Mario, Luigi and Princess Peach. She knew he was impossible, that they all were. Of that, she was sure.

"Where are your parents?" she repeated to the boy kneeling beside her.

He just shook his head and then turned toward the others. They were still and quiet in the plastic chairs. "Bring a broom for the glass would you, Todd? And then you should all go out on the swings."

"Swings!" A little boy, he could only be three, popped up from his seat. His animated little face, excited and adorable, stilled the fear in Emily's body. He wore a pair of seersucker overalls with a strange sort of Christmas patterned vest that was much too hot for summer. He tugged on the hand of a girl, about ten Emily guessed, and they skipped from the room together into the dark corridor.

Todd was the last one. He was about the same age as the boy beside her, but he was chubbier and more sullen. He wore a simple hand sewn shirt, white but impeccably clean, and a pair of slacks tied at the top with a fraying rope. Todd's eyes darted from Emily to the other boy and then back again. He seemed suspicious and unsure.

"Just the broom Todd, and then you can go with them," the one close to her, the skinny boy, said. The command in his voice startled Emily. He was unnaturally confident. Perhaps this was what made him seem so wrong, so out of place.

Todd obeyed. He went to the closet on the opposite end of the room, the one covered in cut-outs and paintings. He opened it as though he had a thousand times before, like it was his own house she had just broken into. He removed the broom without even a glance, and brought it to them. He set it and the dust pan on one of the tables and then took his exit as the braided girl re-entered. She held a first aid kit.

"We'll get you all taken care of." The girl kneeled beside the boy. Emily didn't like her. The girls' green eyes were inexplicably timeworn. Her high lace collar framed her grin. She looked as though she wanted to laugh but was holding the urge in.

The boy took the kit from the girl. "I've got this Angie. You go watch 'em."

Angie nodded thoughtfully. She said nothing as she stood and took a last lingering look at the bloody sight beneath her.

Emily and the boy in charge were left alone. He took her hands and helped her sit up. He brushed some glass from her lap onto the floor and pushed it expertly with the side of his hand into a pile. She could hear only the sound of her own ragged breathing. The boy ripped the top of an antiseptic wipe with his teeth and then swiped it on her right hand, the one she had used to break the window. Her knuckles were shredded and red. The sting brought her back to the moment, back to the absurdity of it all in a sharp second.

"How old are you?" Emily watched as he ripped open another wipe and rubbed it up her left arm, covered in small cuts.

"Uh, well, I'm six." The sides of his lips curled as though he had just told a joke. Emily supposed she must have looked comical to the children. A fat woman smashed through the window and rolled through glass in front of them. She was curious why they weren't more scared of her intrusion.

Emily pushed his hand away from her injured arm. "Where is your mom?" she demanded. "Or teachers? Where are the teachers? Or someone? Are there summer classes now?"

The boy in the Mario Brothers shirt considered this. He rocked on his heels, looking into Emily's eyes with intense curiosity.

"You're not supposed to be in here. It's July and the doors are locked," she continued.

The boy nodded in agreement of her chastisement. She watched his features change. His scrunched eyebrows relaxed and his eyes twinkled.

"Let's go get ice cream down at Fox Lake," he suggested. His cheeks flushed with excitement and his smile was sincerely adorable.

Emily touched her left side gingerly. Her white t-shirt had small blooms of blood that seemed to be growing. "I think maybe I should go to the hospital."

"No." He stood and put his hands out in a gesture to help her up from her corner of the floor. "You're going to be okay."

Emily believed him. His brown eyes told the truth. They were bright and youthful and innocent, yet they were wise eyes. She let the bony six-year-old help her up. His little hands pulled her to standing and she leaned on his sharp shoulder for support. Her sides were on fire, and she was sure she had a gash on the top of her heaving breasts.

Her arms stung and her entire right hand was swollen and throbbing. He was so tiny and she was so hefty, but he seemed to have the strength to help her. The boy led her from the twins' classroom and into the main hall. All the other classrooms were closed and silent. Emily saw no evidence of the other children. They got to the front door and the boy pushed it open. She wondered how that was possible. Sunlight and sticky heat flooded them. Emily pointed to her car and the boy helped her down the cement steps. He was hunched and determined, like a little nurse, Emily mused. They made it to the car and Emily shaded her eyes so she could get a good look at the playground as he helped lower her into the driver's seat. He closed her door with a slam and got in the passenger seat beside her.

"Your friends aren't at the swings, I don't see them." Emily watched as the boy buckled himself in. She wondered if his mother had a booster seat for him, he was so damn skinny. She knew it wasn't right to let him ride in the front. But the sensation of company, of a full car, of a child beside her, forced the practical thoughts from her brain.

"Nah, I'll meet up with them later. Can I get mint chocolate chip, two scoops?" He kicked his stick legs in anticipation.

"Um yeah." Emily started her car and they drove away from Everley. She thought of ice cream then too, and shared his excitement. Maybe it would help the pain, all of the pain.

They drove through the wooded suburb, past the rich houses and the boutiques in silence. They were near the lake; she could see the glimmer of sun on the water. They would have to park on the street, probably a good walk from the ice cream shack. People would see her blood. She hadn't thought much about people and what they would see. She didn't care she was chubby and in sweatpants in front of people, but the blood seemed odd and maybe even a little scary.

"There." The boy pointed to a side street and she turned into a sort of alley between houses. She pulled over, tires on the grass, and parked. "Whatdya want?"

"Hm?" She was looking at her hands.

"Cone or cup?" He slipped underneath the seatbelt without unfastening it.

"Oh cone I guess. Chocolate cherry." Emily hadn't had an ice cream cone since her before life.

"M'kay, I'll be back." He jumped out, slammed the door and was gone. She wondered vaguely if he had money, but decided it really didn't matter. Nothing mattered. She had someone to eat ice cream with, and that felt good. Emily leaned her head back and closed her eyes. She thought of Fiona and Sophie. They would have liked her new friend. They would have chased him on the beach and they could have made sandcastles together.

She would ask him what his name was when he came back. Sammy Overland. His name is Sammy.

Emily's eyes shot open and she lurched forward in her seat, grabbing the steering wheel as though she was drowning and it was her life preserver.

"Sammy Overland," she said to the empty car. His bony knees, those deep brown eyes, and wearing that Mario shirt with a grinning Princess Peach in the background. She started the car up in order to feel the familiar air blast on her face.

No. No. No. No. No.

Emily's entire being trembled with the realization. Vomit began to rise in her throat; she struggled to keep it down. She kept thinking of his school picture, in black and white on the front page, and the color one, the one they gave all of them as reference. Sammy was posing with his big sister. They were in front of their bikes, each with a helmet and matching wide, toothy grins. Sammy was wearing the Mario shirt, his sister's arm curved around his waist.

"Sam was wearing this exact outfit the last afternoon he was seen," the man had said. He was a cop she supposed, but he was in civilian clothes. They had all passed the picture around, the entire group, all hoping they wouldn't find what they were looking for.

And they hadn't.

He came back up the alleyway, a cone in each hand. She watched him lick at the chocolate drips on his bare arm while he made his way back to her. He waited at the passenger door for her to let him in. She couldn't. Her swollen hands, now crusted with drying blood, were limp and cold. Emily could only stare at the impossible boy as he struggled with the door latch.

He finally opened the door and slipped in, breathing heavily. He must have run back here. Emily thought feebly. He tried to hand Emily her cone, but she remained motionless.

Sammy began to lick his own treat and placed hers, with a messy splat, into the console. In her before life Emily would have screeched with disbelief at the ice cream smeared into the cup holder. But now of course she cared little about mess. Her own feet were covered in burger wrappers, pop cans and the caramel wrappers. And too, she was rather occupied by the sick churn in her stomach.

Sammy looked at her face then. He smiled knowingly, just like that girl at the school, the one in braids with the smirk.

"Oh," he said plainly. He placed a cold, sticky hand on her wrist and patted gently. "It's okay."

Nothing had been okay for a very long time. Life had been upside down and backwards and wrong. Yet Emily believed the six year old chewing on a sugar cone in her car. For the first time in years, she was sure everything might be okay.

"I don't understand." She managed confusedly. "I went looking for you, I was a volunteer, up in the woods, we had those dogs, you know those one that smell your pillow. And we had these poles to poke around the bushes. I was so scared."

Sammy nodded.

"That was, God… God that was nearly fifteen years ago. I was in college." Emily watched Sammy Overland finish his treat.

She had cried for him all those years ago, alone in her car, after she saw his mother at the search. Emily wasn't a mother then, but she had recognized the damage in Donna Overland's face, the irrevocable pain.

Sammy smiled, green mint ice cream on his cheeks. He rubbed his belly in satisfaction and then turned to consider Emily next to him.

"Angie says we're like those people in the background of a movie, we're just like shapes and colors and stuff. You all sort of know we're there, but don't remember us, don't really see us. I saw my sister once; she's all big now and has long hair. She was at the rec center, where we used to go swim together, and she has kids now, which is cool. One was even named after me." Sammy giggled at the memory. "She looked right through me, I was swimming with my friends and she didn't really see us, you know? Cause we're just like here, but not. That's how it works I guess. It's okay though." The boy shrugged and settled back into the seat. It seemed as though he thought this explained it all, as though his peculiar words could make sense.

"You swim at the rec center?" Emily asked. It was an odd question, but the only one she could form.

"Yep. Oh, all the time. And we play school like you saw us doing, before, well before you did that," Sammy motioned to her bleeding sides. "We eat lots of ice cream too, or whatever we like. And we go to the Fox Lake playground and sometimes we make tree houses and feed the birds. We get to go anywhere we had fun before, even like Disney and stuff, you know wherever we went in our before life."

Emily felt a tear, and then another, fall onto her fat cheeks. She bowed her head, letting herself cry fully, deeply.

He let her sob into her hands for a few strange moments and then Sammy whispered, "them too."

She looked up from her curtain of stringy hair. "Them too?"

"They play school with us all the time. They like to be the teachers together."

Emily stopped crying. Her body stilled. The vomit settled and she took in an enormous breath. She wanted to hug him. But before she could lean forward he had opened the door and jumped from the seat with a youthful, fluid ease.

"We're gonna eat s'mores tonight and tell spooky stories, so I better go." He picked at an errant splotch of ice cream on his Mario shirt. There was no sadness in his eyes, no indication of the horror story he had lived. There was only joy.

Emily watched Sammy Overland, still skinny and six, slam the car door once more and then skip down the length of the alley and disappear around the corner. He gave one last absentminded wave before he was gone.

She let herself remember the good days at Fox Lake. Emily thought of evening strolls with Adam when her stomach swelled with babies, and later the afternoons they spent with the girls, pink and sticky with Popsicle juice, in the cool water. She let all the good memories come at once.

For the first time in her after life, Emily felt as though she had something to do. She stared at the ice cream melting beside her and felt an urge to clean it. But first she would go to the hospital and get stitched up. She would need some heavy bandages. Then she would find Donna Overland. She was an advocate for missing children and had a rather public profile, so she wouldn't be hard to find. They could have a long chat about their before lives, and their after lives, too. Emily turned on the radio and let the music fill her car. For the first moment in a very long time she didn't feel hungry. There was no rumble in her stomach, no weak, indefinable ache. She forgot all about lunch.

A Flash of Orange

She would have to tell everyone Brian wasn't coming. They would think it was something simple. They would assume he was stuck at the hospital working a holiday shift or perhaps pale and febrile under a quilt at home. The truth would shock them.

"Brian and I broke up," she told the empty car. "So he's not coming to Thanksgiving." It helped to say it aloud, to hear her own voice confirm the truth. She knew when she said it at the snowy threshold of her parents' home, still holding her duffel bag and the store bought pumpkin pie, her mother would shake her head and refuse to believe it.

"Lou," her mother would put a chubby hand on her daughter's shoulder, "this is all temporary I'm sure! Don't worry dear, he'll take you back."

He was the successful one. He was the well-mannered, charming man she had been with since he was a boy. Since she was a girl. They had fallen in love in high school, as children do. And then one particularly cold day in November, he sat her down on the end of their marital bed and explained to her, rather calmly, that he had fallen in love with a man.

She told herself she would keep it a secret from her family for their own good. They believed he was the best thing to ever happen to her, that Brian had pulled their awkward teenage daughter out of her dark bedroom and made her a functional adult.

Louise supposed they were right. So she felt it selfish to tell the truth.

She didn't like driving up north. She was used to being the passenger, feet on the dash and a lukewarm coffee propped on her chest. Last year she had fallen asleep watching the fluffy snow smudge her window. Now the sky was steel gray. There had been freezing rain for the last several miles. She concentrated on the road ahead so hard her hands locked around the steering wheel like claws.

The sky was darkening rapidly. She pushed down the handle to make the wipers go full blast. It didn't help. The icy rain hardened on her windshield. Louise slowed to a crawl, unable to see more than a few feet ahead. She wished she was already there. She didn't look forward to the faces and whispers, but she was desperate to get off the road and be on her parent's sofa with a glass of egg nog with Addy, her eager and plump little niece, on her lap.

At this rate, chugging along on the slickened snow, she wouldn't be there for another twenty agonizing minutes.

The color came then. The flash of orange in the greyish black. She almost slammed her foot onto the brake, it was instinct after all, but she pumped the brake instead, as her father had taught her. She spun only a little, just enough of a rotation to sicken her stomach. Her hands pressed into the steering wheel even deeper.

"Shit!" She hissed. Her belly lurched and turned. Her body shook as she pulled the lever to park.

The car was now across both lanes of the deserted road. Louise was thankful she was on her familiar County Road 21, desolate and quiet. No semi would be pushing through the freezing rain to run her over.

She caught her breath and then willed her quivering legs to get out and see what possible thing had been bright orange and walking across the road in the bitter night. And it was night. The dim rays of twilight had bled away in just a few icy minutes.

Louise unbuckled and stepped into the blackness. Although she wore her sensible wool coat and solid boots, the freezing rain was still able to sting her cheeks and bare hands. She adjusted her faux-fur hat over her straight, raven black hair. The headlights of her Toyota illuminated the woods lining the road. There was nothing but dead trees and blackened, dirty snow.

The hunter was to her left, sitting near the ditch. She first saw the strips of reflective tape on his orange vest; they twinkled in the eerie light. She then saw his figure, sort of slumped but still upright. Steamy breaths puffed from his mouth.

"Oh my God! Did I hit you?!" Louise ran to him, into the dark. The man shook his head but his movement seemed slow and stunned. "Did I hurt you?" She kneeled beside him.

"No, no. I'm okay." The hunter was slender with a gaunt face and bulging eyes. His camouflage hat, lined with fleece, was pulled down over his ears.

"If I was going any faster, Jesus…" Louise steadied herself on her bent legs. "Can I help you up?" She reached out to him.

He looked into her eyes and then pressed his lips together. "Ummmmmmm."

She was afraid he had had a stroke or a concussion. "Sir?"

The hunter took in an enormous breath and then leaned back as though he were in his favorite armchair and not in a mound of dirty slush. "Where's Brian?"

"Excuse me?" Louise had the sudden urge to stand up. But she didn't.

The hunter cupped his gloved hands around his lips and yelled toward Louise's empty car "BRIAN! BRIAN YOU STUPID FUCKER! YOU IN THEREEEE?"

Louise fell on her ass. She felt the ice through her jeans. "What?" Her sick stomach had returned as though she was spinning once more.

"I don't think Brian's in there." The skinny man in the orange vest mused to himself. "I don't think he is."

Louise tried to find purchase on the ice and snow. She tried to dig her heels into the snow and push her body up. But the hunter leapt forward like a spider. He was on top of her before she could scream.
Louise tasted his musty glove as he shoved his fingers into her mouth. The hunter pushed down on her throat with his other hand as she kicked and wiggled. He was thin but strong. Blackness, even darker than the November night, clouded her sight. She tried to look up at his face, into his eyes. She thought perhaps, as her mind slipped away, there would be an answer in his eyes.

~

Her mind came back. At first she could think only of her tongue, fuzzy and swollen. Then she felt her wrists. They were bound together in front of her with a sort of rope that rubbed her cold skin raw. The frayed twine even left a red mark on her belly where it burned like itchy fire. Louise carefully sat up on a mattress. She was in a room with no windows. It was an unfinished space with no drywall and an uneven cement floor. She blinked furiously at the battery powered lantern on the floor. It was so bright after so much dark.

She smelled nothing. The air was cold and sterile. Her checkered wool coat was gone. Her high heeled boots were gone too. Louise wore only her tan bra and her pair of pink panties with bursts of blue flowers on the butt. She shivered.

She would not think of the scrawny hunter undressing her while she was unconscious. She would think about that later when there was room in her brain.

There was a door. It looked brand new with a glistening brass door knob. Louise struggled to stand on the lumpy mattress. She used her elbows to push herself up. Her clasped hands were red and hot from the rope's pressure.

Louise considered not opening the door. At least in her cold room there were no shadows or men in orange vests. But her cautiousness was out ruled by her overwhelming desire to run. She would run on her bare feet until there was light, until there were people, until she was home.

She struggled with her bound hands. It opened. She was in another unfinished room, this one full of boxes and furniture stacked high. Louise navigated through the maze of junk, making out the handwritten words in sharpie on the cardboard: BOOKS, MISC, JOHN'S CDs.

A small hint of light filtered through the snow on several small, rectangular basement windows. There were stairs. Louise took each step slowly. They were old and creaked underneath her bare feet. After each groan of wood, she would stop and listen for someone upstairs to move. But she only heard her own ragged breath.

As she reached the top step, the last one before another door with a brass handle, she steeled herself for the reality of what was beyond. The hunter would be waiting with a gun, a big rifle for shooting deer; or he would have a knife, which was worse. He would be sitting patiently, waiting for her to walk right to him. Maybe he was behind her now, doing his spider crawl up the stairs.

It was a kitchen. Empty. There was a living room too. The walls were knotty pine and the glass doors went out to a deck that overlooked an enormous, frozen lake. She surveyed the rooms as quickly as she could, the smell of fire filling her nose. The fireplace was crackling. She skittered to it and warmed her swollen hands and chilled feet.

The fire meant of course that he was close. She crouched down in front of the flames. Her mind had never stretched so infinitely. She thought of a million things, images of guns, knives, headlights, teeth and snow soaking her jeans. She thought of her niece Addy coloring on her grandfather's desk; she thought of her wedding veil tucked in her own dark curls; she thought of Brian driving as she watched the snow. She was going to die, and before her death that hunter was going to touch her. She tasted his knit glove once again. Louise believed she would taste that stale glove for the rest of her short life.

There was something in the fireplace. Amidst the firewood there was burning material. Louise stared into the orange flame. Her wool coat was nearly gone, but the heels of her boots were easy to make out. They were melting in a pile of what she expected were her charred jeans.

Louise backed away from the heat. There was a large family photo above the driftwood like mantle. It was the typical family pose done at a department store studio. Two girls in ponytails stood behind their mom and dad, little hands awkwardly cupping their parent's shoulders. Louise stared at the mother. She had blushed apple cheeks and round trusting eyes. The father was thin of course.

A recipe box sat on the coffee table. It was odd, Louise noted, because the house was perfectly organized. There were no sloppy stacks of mail on the kitchen counter or dolls stuffed into the couch cushions. Every book and trinket had a place. But, she realized, that was because she was in a cabin, not a house. A tidied and organized summer cabin in the grip of winter.

She tried to pick up the box with her twisted hands but instead managed to drop the contents all over the hearth rug. Her driver's license had landed face up, her own happy and oblivious face smiling for the flash. Seven more plastic cards lay before her. She crouched down to look at them, straining to read the small writing in the firelight. An Asian girl, Flora Li the block letters read, stared up with an expression of boredom. She was 5'1 and her license had expired.
Louise swallowed hard.

"Jaclyn Emory." Louise couldn't hold the license for a better look, but she could recognize the fiery red hair and expanse of freckles on Jaclyn's nose anywhere. Jaclyn Emory's image was on countless newscasts. She had disappeared in the last year, not far from Louise's childhood farm. The police found Jaclyn's car in a ravine, empty and wiped of fingerprints.

Louise thought instantly of her car, how the headlights illuminated nothing but dirty snow and scratchy bushes. She wondered where it was now, if it was tucked onto a back road or a sloping gulch with a clean steering wheel.

Brian. The hunter had known Brian, and he had known her somehow. He had screamed her husband's name. She pushed herself up off the floor and forced her eyes to the family portrait over the mantle once more.

Louise didn't want to look at his little girls and his wife again. She studied the hunter's face, his sunken cheeks and protruding front teeth.

She did know him. He and his family were vacationers. They, like so many others, spent their summers on the lake and then returned home to the suburbs or the big city, not hearty enough to handle the Northern winters.

She had a vague memory of him in town. It had been summer and the hunter wore khaki shorts, holding a paper bag of groceries with one hand and petting her parent's pug with the other. He talked clumsily to her father while she and Brian stopped into the liquor store for a bottle of cheap wine.

Brian mocked the hunter in a careful whisper, "Look at your dad, he looks like he wants to run!" He then curled up his front lip and stuck out his teeth to resemble the man. Louise gave her husband an indulgent smile while she watched the conversation from the window. Her dad's pug, Biscuit, certainly hadn't growled or bit the hunter as he patted her with his spindly fingers.

As Louise backed away from the fire burning her clothes, she thought dogs were supposed to sense evil and warn humans. But she couldn't blame Biscuit could she? Louise tried to help the hunter in the orange vest. She had leant down and extended her hand. Louise hadn't considered a man could hurt her any more than Brian had. But her throbbing hands, raw from the rope, were an indication she was in for a world of inconceivable pain.

She couldn't help wondering why the hunter had targeted her. Did he know Brian had made fun of him? Had she sealed her fate with complicit silence? But most striking of all was that the women in the licenses were different. While Jaclyn was slight and freckled, Louise had her father's tanned, powerful legs and deep brown Ojibwa eyes. She inherited all her father's native traits as though her own mother had not contributed a single bit of DNA. Then there was tiny Flora Li. They were all so physically different; Louise had to believe that there was a clue in their disparities. Perhaps he was not only a hunter, but a collector too.

Her throat was hoarse. Her neck was sore on either side, as though she had slept on it wrong. But, of course, she hadn't really slept. She had blacked out from being choked. She would think about that later, she would stuff that realization into her back pocket for another day.

Louise stopped stretching the muscles in her neck. There was a crunch on the far side of the cabin. It was outside, the unmistakable sound of a foot in snow. Then another step, slow and deliberate. She felt instantly vulnerable, standing in the middle of the living room in her undies and a rope around her hands.

She trembled at the sound. Her mind wanted to distract her. She wanted to believe it was the cabin settling into the snow or perhaps a fallen icicle. But then a horrific wail so grotesquely unbelievable, seeped through the walls.

"Wahhhh….WHAAAAAAA…." It was barely human.

Louise stood perfectly still. She could sense her heart thumping against her breast like a caged bird.

There was more crunching in the snow, characterized by a slow dragging between steps. Louise had a flash of *The Shining*. She could think only of dead eyed Jack Nicholson dragging behind his axe in the icy maze. That image cracked through her brain and she found the bravery to run to the front door. She snapped the deadbolt across with her few useful fingers. Louise knew the hunter would have a key to his own cabin, but the feeling of the deadbolt under her grip was calming nonetheless.

"Heeeeyyy…..ahhhhhh…..HEEEEYYYYY" The moaning was louder now, closer to the door. Louise had to look. There was a front window with dark green curtains obstructing the light and her view. She pushed one curtain aside, just a few inches, and peeked out into the front yard. The sun hitting the fresh snow created a blinding effect, so at first she saw nothing but pure light. As her eyes adjusted, she saw the hunter.

He wasn't charging around the cabin with weapon in hand as she had imagined. He was crawling on his belly making his way from the side of the cabin around toward the front. He used his stick arms to drag himself in the soft, deep snow. Louise vaguely wondered how long she had actually been on the dirty mattress. It had snowed a considerable amount since the ice storm.

He was perhaps a foot in front of the window and he was covered in blood.

She thought of Jaclyn Emory and the Asian girl, Flora. Was it their blood on his face? In his hair?

Louise trembled behind the flimsy curtain. There was just a pane of glass between her and the hunter. But he was slowing. She stared at his lower body. One leg was shredded, the meat hanging like pulled pork. His foot was simply gone. His orange vest was now crimson with an occasional white puff of cotton spilling out of a few deep gashes.

The hunter looked as though he were a swimmer, one out his depth and about to drown. He did a forward stroke in the snow while pushing with his good foot. His only foot. Louise was very sure he had had two feet while he sat on the side of County Road 21.

He gasped for air and then gave another lamenting moan. He had left a long streak of blood in the snow behind him, farther than Louise could even see. It was a bizarre trail, like the kind a snail leaves behind, yet this one was bright red.

The hunter turned then, perhaps to try a side stroke, but he stopped when he saw her. Their eyes locked. Fear funneled through her, filling her cold flesh with electric fire. But as quickly as it came, it oozed out of her pores. It was not Flora's blood on his teeth or bubbling out of his mouth. It was not Jaclyn's blood. It was not her own blood. Louise smiled at the realization. The stretch of her mouth pained her injured throat, but she didn't care. She was watching the hunter die.

"Heeeeey….hey…..hell…..HELLPP!..." He coughed red into the snow. Louise pushed her face to the glass, showcasing her smile. "Biii….BITCH!" He gurgled.

He murdered women. She was sure of that. So she enjoyed watching him die. She didn't think of her own pain, but of the seven other licenses she had found. The strange trophies he had kept to remember the others. Her heart sank at the thought of their deaths. They were probably buried underneath the snow, or perhaps they were weighted down into the lake, the same lake his daughters splashed in on summer vacations.

The hunter moved one last time. His three working limbs seemed to stiffen at once. His jaw clamped down while blood flowed from his nose. He died with his eyes open.

Louise watched his body for what felt like hours. She had to make sure he was dead. She couldn't go out there and feel his claw around her ankle. She couldn't be pulled down into the bloody snow.

She could see now he had something in one of his hands. It was a red stick with some sort of charred ash on the top. It looked similar to a road flare Louise had in her car's emergency kit. Not that she would ever know how to use one. She wondered why he bothered to carry a burned out flare in his final moments on Earth.

The dull ache in her wrists returned as she finally backed away from the window. Her mind began to spin again. She thought of her parents, surely worried by now, and she thought of her boots in the crackling fire. Louise was at once happy to be alone, free of the hunter, but also terrified of the loneliness. She couldn't do this on her own.

Louise hesitated. She couldn't trust herself. She couldn't do it. She couldn't make a choice, a decision, an action.

But perhaps she had to. Louise caught a reflection of herself in a mirror at the end of the hall. Her panties sagged and her belly protruded. She had let herself go, she supposed, as married people do. But she wasn't going to be a married person for much longer; she was not half of anything anymore. Brian had done everything for her. He had shielded his young wife from the world. He had done the hard things, the things she didn't want to do. He made the appointments and paid the bills and took out the trash. Worst of all, she had let him.

But now she was nearly naked, tied up and alone. More alone than she had ever known was possible. Her smartphone was surely gone, simmering in the same fire as her other belongings. Her car was gone, and she hadn't seen a vehicle in the driveway.

She knew once she started moving she wouldn't be able to stop. She would have to let the part of her brain, the resourceful piece she had rarely used, take control. The cabin had no phone. There were no visible neighbors through the dead trees, and, even if there were more lake cabins close by, they would be empty this time of year.

Louise went through the closets in the two bedrooms with her useless hands. There were no clothes. She found a pair of swimming goggles, a pile of forgotten stuffed animals and a collection of dusty Ann Rule paperbacks.

"How ironic," she muttered under her breath. It hurt to talk.

There was nothing sharp to cut the rope. She checked the silverware drawer in the kitchen and found only white, plastic sporks. It had taken her five tries just to get the drawer open with her pinkie. Rage bubbled in her stomach.

She would be angry later. Now she needed something for her feet. A patchwork blanket sat on the back of the couch. It looked hand crocheted, probably a few decades ago based on the yellow and orange yarn.

There was a garage. She had studied the side of it as she waited for the dead man's resurrection. Thankfully he had never resurrected and thankfully too the door on the garage looked to be slightly ajar. Louise steadied herself for the inevitable. She would have to walk in the snow with bare legs, and she would have to walk past the hunter. She opened the deadbolt after a few tries and used her elbows to turn the doorknob. The cold hit her entire body with a bitter slap. She didn't stop. She ran into the fluffy white, her feet numb at first to the ice. As she ran, past the body and over the bloody trail, she thought of the other women and of how much they would have liked to run. How they would have gladly felt the stabbing cold in their legs.

She pushed through the side garage door and reveled in the sight of tools and sharp things. At first, as she gazed over the hunter's garage, she felt the overwhelming feeling she was out of her element. That this was where her good ideas would end. She would die in the fetal position on the frozen cement floor because she couldn't reason, couldn't organize her thoughts. Instead she took in a deep breath and summoned the maturity and the courage she had wanted all along.

There was a chainsaw resting on a work bench. She tried to rub the rope against the blade, but it was too dull. She then found a knife, she thought maybe it was called a bowie knife, and pinched it between her middle fingers. With concentration and precision she dropped the handle into a vice on the side of the workbench. She tightened the vice with her mouth. The metal reminded her of the unwelcome taste of his gloves. Once tightened she rubbed the rope on the upturned blade and it popped off. She took one second to flex her fingers and roll her wrists. She had accomplished something.

Her legs burned in the snow as she ran back to the cabin. Louise thought it was odd that her skin could be so cold that it felt as though it was red-hot. It was just too much for her nerves to take.

She skidded back into the living room on wet feet and grabbed the throw blanket. She had brought the knife with her and now used it to cut the bottom of the blanket into strips. Louise tied the pieces of yarn around each foot. Then she took the remaining blanket and put it over her shoulders and tied it around her throbbing neck. Louise had a faint idea of taking the hunter's clothes. But they were bloody and she would have to touch him. And he only had one boot.

She took the thick top comforter off what was probably the hunter's bed and tried to fashion a sort of bizarre ball gown around her legs. It kept slipping as she attempted to tie it around her middle. She couldn't help but think of the old Carol Burnett sketch, the one where Carol's Scarlett O'Hara creates a makeshift dress from curtains and happens to leave the rod in the shoulders. Louise actually laughed.

Before she left she picked up every license from the floor. She tucked them into her panties, and the last few into her bra, including her own.

Louise thought only of running. She ran, her feet instantly frozen with only her crude yarn shoes to cover them. She sprinted down the sloping hill toward the lake, the blanket flapping behind like a cape. The comforter only inhibited her running, so she reluctantly left it behind in a sad slump on the front lawn.

It wasn't until the cabin was out of view, she remembered the hunter's shredded leg. It wasn't until she was in the woods, alone and cold, she realized something had happened to the hunter. What had eaten his foot?

"Fuck, fuck…," Louise panted. She hunched over and put her hands on her bare knees. A small plastic card fell from her bra into the snow. She picked it up, vaguely aware of how her legs were now bright red from the cold. Louise wanted to look at the image. She wanted to see who had come before her, who had done their turn at the hunter's cabin. But she tucked it in her bra again without looking. She just couldn't do it now. Not now.

She took a dramatically deep breath. Her chest felt as though it had filled with brittle icicles and her heart thudded dully underneath. But she felt an incredible strength. There was a necessity to her life; she had to deliver the licenses.

Louise ran once more, slower now but more determined. She was surrounded by dense woods and the gleam of the frozen lake beside her.

The knife.

She had left the knife on the couch. She had thought only of leaving, of running. She didn't think of the blood trail and red bubbles between his lips.

"Something ate his foot." Louise told the trees. She heard only a crack of a branch heavy with snow in return.

Although the snow was thick, she could sense a decline underneath her. She was coming down the side of a hill and had to begin holding onto the trunks of trees to aid her balance. Her legs felt like jelly and she knew soon they would lose their tingle and she would feel nothing. Then they would turn another color, blue perhaps, and then finally black.

Her legs felt gelatin and tingly when Brian sat her down that afternoon in their apartment, which, now, felt so long ago.

"I'm in love with Scott, Lou, we're in love with each other."

Louise thought of them as she slipped onto her butt, the decline becoming steeper. She imagined her husband was with Scott at this very moment. Scott, the pediatric nurse who she had considered her friend, who had come to their holiday party last year with an ironic fruit cake and a Scrabble board under his arm. It wasn't the sex that made her shudder. It was the images of the mundane, of Brian bringing his new love, a cup of coffee with the milk and sugar, already stirred, of him taking out Scott, the nurse's, recycling. Those were the thoughts that haunted her.

His foot.

There it was. It was waiting for her where the hill was beginning to flatten out. She hadn't noticed a blood trail on the hill; it had gone off in a different direction, a less treacherous short cut to the cabin she supposed. But there the boot sat, upright as though the hunter had simply stepped out of it. Although it was covered in dried blood, there was no flesh sticking out. Louise was thankful for that. There was something white that could be bone, but she looked away as she walked toward it. She gazed up at the sky, clouded but still bright.

She made sure to give the foot a wide berth. It scared her there, bloody and silent. Louise walked on. She noticed the woods were thinning, there were less trees and the snow was becoming dirtier.

"A road," she croaked. Her body was almost entirely frozen now. She was losing feeling in her hands and she knew her legs would not carry her for much longer. Yet her throat still throbbed.

The road was paved and had recently been plowed as evidenced by the black showing through the snow. She crawled up the embankment feeling as though she had emerged from Hell itself. Her body was giving way, crumbling beneath her. She clawed her way up onto the curb. There was no rumble of a truck or a family van, not yet, but she knew someone would have to come. They would have to.

She was done. She made sure she would be visible but not road kill. She lay down. It began to snow on her face, the big white puffs she had favored so ardently from the safety of her car. She raised a limp, feeble hand over her eyes as a shield.

The world was silent. Her mind flitted from one idea to the next. Louise thought of the Thanksgiving dinner she had missed. She thought of Brian and Scott at the mall, holding hands and choosing a place for lunch. She thought of the flash of orange.

And then she was not alone. She could feel it before she could hear it. There was a presence. For one horrible second she imagined it was the hunter. He had squirmed down the hill behind her and was now here to eat her foot. Fair was fair.

She forced herself to raise her chin and look down the road. She thought it was a dog at first. Not Biscuit of course, it was too large. She surprised herself by sitting up rather quickly.

The dog was not a dog. It was a timber wolf. She had seen one at the Minnesota Zoo before, on the Northern Trail exhibit, and she had seen a few, far off, up by the farm. But the one on the road, a few yards from her feet had red dripping from its mouth. It was a statue. Even its yellow eyes stared at her without a blink or a flutter.

Her father taught her to respect wolves. He told her wolves were somehow predictors of their tribe's future. If bad things came to the wolves then bad things would befall her and her loved ones. There was a kinship, a brotherhood she had always felt with the wolves. But now, now she was only scared.

Another wolf, larger than the first, padded down the hill Louise had just traversed and jumped the curb with a fluid ease. He raised his considerable snout and sniffed the air. Except for the glistening red gore on their jaws, both wolves were the color of muddied snow.

Louise felt the plastic cards in the back of her panties, nudging her along. She rose slowly, aware that her feet were indeed turning a cerulean blue.

She watched the wolves. They were still motionless, but now emitted a low frequency growl she could barely hear.

Louise walked backward while holding both palms up as though she were a crook cornered by the police. She took each step carefully, her eyes focused on their curled lips.

The bigger one had something wrong with his face. There was exposed pink skin where there should be fur. He had been injured, burned perhaps.

The flare. The flare in his hand. He had probably been struggling with it to get it started as they ate his foot.

The smaller one placed a tentative paw forward. Before she could process its movement, the wolf was running toward her, its swinging tail a hypnotic pendulum. She watched the snarling monster come closer. Then the other one, the one with the burns, came bounding forward too and her brain unseized. She had to run, she had to keep running.

Louise turned and started down the road on her dying feet. She wondered if she could climb up a tree, if her body could manage it, but as the idea danced across her mind she saw a pick-up truck parked on the side of the embankment with the driver's door gaping open like a forgotten task.

They were behind her, gaining on her, she was sure she could feel their hot breath on the back of her ice legs. She felt an incredible pain on her sore neck as a ripping sound filled her ears. It was the blanket, the homemade afghan stitched by the hunter's grandmother surely, that was being ripped off her neck and torn aside. She looked over her shoulder for one brief peek and saw one of the wolves rolling about, tangled in the knitting like an animal caught in a trap. The other nipped at her heels as she leapt inside the rusted pick-up. Louise scrambled into the driver's seat. She tried to reach for the door handle but the wolf's head appeared in the open space and chomped down onto Louise's left calf as she struggled to close the door.

Her scream was one of rage and frustration. She didn't scream in pain. Louise couldn't feel the punctures in her numb leg. The pain would come later. It all would.

She surprised herself with her strength. She shook her legs wildly, but the wolf didn't let go. His buddy was now untangled from the blanket and had sidled up to the pickup truck, waiting for his turn to gnaw on her leg. She thought of the single boot in the snow.

"GET OFF!" She punched the wolf in one yellow eye. The animal yelped. It was the same cry of an injured dog. The sound made Louise hesitate. But as she pulled her arm back for another punch, she began to feel the pain, feel the teeth in her leg. She could sense the gushing blood beginning to warm her frozen limbs.

"GO AWAY!" She hit with all her power, all that was left, and the wolf reeled back, unhinging its jaw from her leg. She didn't wait to watch it react. Instead she slammed the truck door closed and reveled in the sound of the two wolves scratching on the side. They could not have her foot.

She turned the keys dangling in the transmission before she even considered how odd it was that they were there for her taking. The truck started. The purr of the engine was magnificent. This was the hunter's truck. There was a coil of rope on the passenger seat, the same that had been around her wrists. And the hunter's own license was in a brown, leather wallet tucked in the console. She didn't put that one with the others. But she placed the wallet on her naked legs and began to drive. The wolves yapped after her like a pair of frustrated Chihuahuas.

Louise came across County Road 21. The white and black sign was a beacon of hope, a reminder that the world had not spun out of orbit. She drove past a family with a Christmas tree strapped on the roof of their car. This made her very happy.

She made it to her parent's farm and parked the hunter's truck between two state trooper vehicles. She told herself she just had a few more steps, just a few more and then she could rest.

Louise walked up onto the front porch and pulled the door open. The entry way was empty, except for a large pile of shoes which Louise regretfully bled all over as she stepped into the living room. Her mother was on the couch, her head buried in her father's chest. A police officer sat in the chair opposite, taking notes on his iPad. Her brother leaned against the mantle, a cup of steaming coffee in his hand. They all sensed her presence and stared with wide eyes as she entered the room.

"This man," Louise gasped as she motioned toward the wallet in her hand, "....this man killed lots of women. He killed Flora Li and Jaclyn Emory."

Louise dropped the wallet on the floor and began removing the plastic cards from her bra and panties. "But don't worry because his foot was eaten by wolves."

The police officer stood in shock. Her brother set his coffee down with a trembling hand. Her mother sniffed away a few tears.

Louise felt her body sink to the floor. Her family jumped forwards, all cradling her before she could bump her head on the hardwood. She looked up at her parents' inquisitive faces.

"Oh also…" The edges of Louise's vision were beginning to darken. She knew her mind would have a nice rest very soon. "Brian is gay. Or something." She could feel relief spreading through her veins. "He's in love with Scott."

Louise's mother patted her daughter's icy forehead. "Shhh."

"No, it's okay Mom, it's really okay because I think I'm going to be alright on my own."

Louise slept. Through the darkness, she heard the sirens whirring toward the farm. She listened and felt pleased. Pleased that the taste of the hunter's glove had left her, ephemeral and forgotten.

The Pit

The first time I committed murder I was six years old. I knew it was wrong. But my Uncle Jeremy smelled of moldy leather and dusty cigarettes. He watched us on Wednesday nights, when Mom had her night class at the technical college. That last night he brought us a pizza. It had green peppers on it. He snickered when he told me to pick them out of the hot cheese.

"Ah Missy," he had said when I burned my tiny fingers. "You clumsy nut."

I knew I was going to bring him to The Pit. It was the end of summer and soon it would be impossible to get him there. Here in Minnesota summer changes into fall over one night, there is simply no more warmth and the leaves instantly turn orange. I figured I had only a few decent summer days left.

Jeremy put baby Dawson to bed with a bottle he warmed in the microwave. I had to help him with the buttons; he would have melted the plastic if I hadn't helped. He was drunk of course. There was never a time he wasn't listing to the side and hiccupping like a cartoon character with a jug marked XXX in its paws.

Then I said we should go The Pit. He bent his greasy head back and laughed.

"It's still hot out." I crossed my arms and tightened my brows, so I looked like I was going to cry. Jeremy hated when I cried, he would usually leave me alone with a handful of toilet paper and take a smoke break out on the front porch until I stopped. "And school's coming and it's gonna get cold, this is my last chance."

I watched as he wiped his red nose with the back of his hand. He considered my face, strained and quivering as though I was on the precipice of a tantrum.

"Twenty minutes," he grumbled.

I went into the bathroom and climbed up onto the toilet to reach my swimsuit hanging on the shower rod. It was still damp from when Dawson and I had gone to The Pit that afternoon. I took off my nightgown, the one with the ponies jumping over a fluorescent rainbow on the front, and left it in a pile with my undies. I looked in the mirror as I raked my brown hair back into a bun. I knew it was murder because I was looking into my own eyes and not stopping. As I stood in the cramped bathroom of our tiny bungalow on River Street, I knew precisely what I was doing.

We left sleeping Dawson and hiked up the steep hill to The Pit. My flip flops crunched beneath me in the night. Uncle Jeremy carried a plastic shopping bag with my towel inside. The orange glow at the end of the cigarette tucked between his lips was the only light. My eyes grew accustomed to the darkness as we made our way through the wooded gravel path.

Then we arrived. The moon was visible now, and its grey light reflected on the water like a dream. We now had to make our way down the rocky incline to swim.

"We nee' ta be back by ten or your mommy's gonna kill me," Jeremy slurred as he slid down the embankment on his ass. The cigarette didn't fall from his mouth.

I knew he wouldn't get in the water right away. But I had a plan. I slipped my flip flops off and put a cautious toe into the water. I took in the small stretch of shore; there were no teenagers skinny-dipping or night strollers walking their dogs. We were alone. I got in the black water slowly as he watched from the rocks. I waded out to the middle of The Pit. It was very deep, endlessly deep. The Pit was named for its past as a mining pit, iron ore, before it was stripped bare and flooded. Some of us locals swim in The Pit. We like to avoid the tourist lakes with the rental boats and the overpriced pop.

I got all the way up to my neck before I felt it. The thing in the pit, my thing, caressed my bare legs with its familiar, ghostly fingers. Then it pressed firmer, pleased to see me, and I could feel the tentacles, vaguely sticky and strong around my stomach. It would not hurt me. I knew this from the first time it had tugged at my toes when I was barely four.

It had chosen me when I still had puffy swim diapers under my pink suit. I was scared of the sensation of something underneath the surface touching me at first; I had watched most of *Jaws* on cable with my older cousins. But then there was a warm buzz in my little head; a string of comforting words as it squeezed around me. It understood me. It liked to hear my dark thoughts, the real ugly, bloody ideas that Mom would usually slap me for. She said I couldn't say things like that out loud. My thoughts scared her. But I didn't need to even say them from my mouth to The Pit. Instead my thing would make me feel special for having my thoughts. It loved me.

With a sideways look to make sure Uncle Jeremy was watching, I pretended to struggle. I dipped my head under the surface and pin wheeled my arms as though I couldn't swim. As I bobbed back up, I shouted and writhed rather dramatically. The thing, my thing, unfurled its gentle hold on me; it knew what was happening too.

I could see Uncle Jeremy getting up on his unsteady feet, his stub of a cigarette finally forgotten, falling from his mouth in a fiery streak. He didn't bother to remove his beloved motorcycle boots before he ran into the water.

It was nice he cared. I had the quickest flash of something like regret. This was my last chance to stop. I didn't have to act out my thoughts. But I wanted to.

"Melissa!" He screamed as he doggy paddled toward me. I kept thrashing and coughing and I called his name in return.

"I got you, I got you." He tried to grab my shoulder and that's when I stopped struggling and pushed away. I could never drown in The Pit. The Pit would never let me. The thing inside the water was my buoy keeping me afloat and safe.

Uncle Jeremy waded next to me, his lips began to tighten up and his dark eyes looked stormy. "Is this a joke Missy? Is this a fucking joke?"

He almost seemed sober. I smiled.

Then he felt The Pit too. It must have grabbed him around his ankle because he jerked suddenly and his head was under the water before I could blink. Then he came back up, coughing and snorting for real. I stayed where I was, watching him drown while I lazily kicked my legs to stay upright. I knew The Pit would do what I wanted. It had told me so. It had told me without really talking.

He tried to scream, but there was too much water in his mouth and coming out of his nostrils. He clawed up at the water. Just his hands were above the surface; angry, scratching claws. Then my Uncle Jeremy was gone, pulled underneath. I waited to make sure he didn't come up like a floating cork.

When I got home I put my nightgown on, the same one with the ponies, and wrung out my swimsuit. I put it back on the shower rod and watched TV and ate cold pizza with the peppers pulled off until Mom pushed through the front door and asked where Uncle Jeremy had run off to.

I told her that he said something about meeting a girl on Fox Bluff. She got red and huffed that she would kill him; she would just kill him for leaving me and Dawson alone. I smiled at her; I had already taken care of it.

Seven summers later, Aiden Todd went straight down like an anchor. It had been a hot day and his pale, freckled skin had called to me from the shore. I had been at The Pit alone until Aiden showed up. I spent most every day there. Even when The Pit was bursting with squealing kids and horny teenagers I could find a place to float and be with my Pit. But I preferred to come when it was silent and the water was still. I could share my scattered thoughts, a steady stream of dark ideas. The Pit listened.

But then Aiden, a notorious bully, eased into the water with a pair of goggles swinging from his thick neck. I knew he had pushed my baby brother Dawson into the side of a vending machine on the last day of school. Dawson said Aiden laughed so hard tears dripped down his white cheeks. Now, as he swam towards me, Aiden leered at my burgeoning breasts and made disgusting comments. My Pit thing knew what to do; it clamped onto the bully's chubby legs. He went down, quick and silent.

I had the oddest sensation of jealousy. He was down there with The Pit, in its lair, and I couldn't be.

Six uneventful years went by. I was nineteen when Jake Tuttle asked me to murder again. He didn't know The Pit and I had done it before. We were in my bed, my zebra print sheets all pushed to the end of the mattress. Jake was naked, but I had slipped my panties back up.

"They're going to pin it on me; I'm going to be their prime suspect." He worked a toothpick into his mouth, considering his options. "I've got to have an alibi, Missy, something real solid, like lots of people to say I was there and I couldn't have done it."

"I'll do it." I shrugged.

Jake didn't hear me. "She's a real bitch Missy. She hates me, screams at me, but she wants to get pregnant and trap me."

He felt it necessary to invoke my rage.

"I'll do it tomorrow." I handed him his boxers. "We'll make sure you have an alibi. But you have to get her to The Pit first. Tell her you'll meet here there late, um, let's say midnight. Don't text her about it though. The police will look at your texts."

Jake sat up; his scruffy face a mixture of relief and awe. "How? How will you do it at The Pit?"

I shook my head. "You just get her there and I'll take care of it."

"Are you going to stab her with something?" His words trailed off into a trembling whisper.

"She'll be gone." I kissed Jake on his bare shoulder.

"But Missy," he blinked, "if you're going to weigh her down into the water, like with something heavy, you're going to need me. You're too small." He pulled me into his chest and hugged me roughly to emphasize his point.

"No, no, you go to Dexter's."

"Miss..."

"Jake, I mean it. Just go to Dexter's right after dinner, around eight, and get real loud and invite the boys. Then go home with one of them, sleep on a couch. Oh and you should even flirt with that waitress; you know the one with all the moles on her face."

We laughed. But then I pulled back and watched him. He stared past me, past the window. The toothpick hung from the corner of his mouth, limp, and forgotten.

He didn't think I could do it. I felt angry he didn't trust me, but mostly I was excited to prove him wrong. He kissed me on the forehead before he rolled off the bed and retrieved his work jeans from a puddle of clothes on the floor. I loved Jake. I wanted him for myself although he was married and he drank too much and he smelled of stale cigarettes just as Uncle Jeremy had.

She came down the steep decline very slowly, testing each step with a tentative wiggle. Andrea Tuttle was still in her Taco Bell uniform; black greasy slacks and a white collared shirt. She even had the visor with the recognizable bell stitched in yellow on top of her blonde stringy hair. It was dark and so she couldn't see me wading up to my chin in the deep water. I could feel The Pit stroking my sides, reassuring me. It would help me. It wanted what I wanted.

I was surprised when she started to undress. Andrea shivered as she removed her uniform and left it on the narrow strip of sand. She placed her Taco Bell visor gingerly on top of her pile of clothes as though it were a treasured keepsake. Jake's wife wore a bikini, the kind with string sides that embedded into her fleshy thighs and two tiny triangles that covered a small portion of her swinging breasts.

I thought of her picking the tight bottoms out of her ass crack as she wrapped hard shells in paper and scooped guacamole.

Andrea made her way into The Pit as slowly as she had crept down the hill. Honestly, I thought I was going to have to push her in, or pretend to drown again, or tell her some story about needing her help finding my pearl earring. But I had underestimated her want of Jake; her willingness to trust him.

"Jake?" She was up to her waist, her breasts skimming the water. "Jake you moron," she panted. "You better not scare me. Where the hell are you?" Her eyes were suspicious slits.

I stayed still. The Pit swirled around me. It was nudging my legs like an anxious dog ready for the hunt.

Andrea pushed out a little deeper in to the black water, probably to avoid the chilly wind from hitting her naked back.

"Hi, Andrea!" I bobbed up and gave a dramatic wave.

She startled, twisting her head in every direction to see where my voice came from. I think she saw me, or at least made out my figure, because she began to dog paddle toward me. She thought I was her friend I suppose.

It happened so quickly, even faster than Aiden Todd. She was doing her little doggy kick and then she stopped. Her mouth gaped like a fish on a hook, surprised and angry. Andrea made a little soft sound, the whiny grumble of an indignant child refusing to believe life is indeed not fair. Then she was pulled backward with such force her hair whipped the water and her hands dug into the surface as though she were on a high ledge and she was scrambling for purchase. But of course there was nothing to grab on to and so she sank down. Her hands and feet were in the air like an upturned beetle as her body was drawn into the blackness.

I backstroked in the new silence. After a while I felt The Pit come back to me; the pressure of its arms, its ghostly tentacles, its ephemeral body felt good against mine. I was half asleep, dozing in its embrace when I heard Jake on the shore. I knew he couldn't really be there; he was safe at Dexter's, so I figured it was a dream. I snuggled in closer to the water, ready to imagine it was Jake's arms around me, lifting me up. I wanted to pretend it was Jake's fingers lightly caressing my thighs.

"Pssssst. Psssst Melissa?!" Jake's distinct gravelly voice whispered from the side of The Pit. "Missy?!"

I felt nothing around me, no warmth or embrace. I only could hear Jake's voice, cutting and decidedly real, in the night. *Jake, you moron.*

He jumped in before I could protest. He should be far away, in popular and brightly lit Dexter's bar, playing pool with friends and telling bad jokes.

"Missy is it done?" He was by my side in a few single strokes.

"Jesus shut up." I pushed him. "Someone could walk by."

Jake nodded thoughtfully and put his muscular arms around me. "I'm sorry, is everything okay?"

I couldn't help grinning. "Yeah, everything is good."

We kissed then. He ran his hands all over me and I felt like I made him happy. I was useful. I tucked my head under his chin and I was going to chide him, gently, for not staying put, for leaving his golden alibi, but then his whole body quivered beside me.

I pushed back from him, to watch his expression. Jake's eyebrows were knit together in confusion. He was still floating in the water, but his arms cycled frantically.

No, no, no.

"Jake, c'mon, let's get out, let's get out." My voice was shaky. I stretched out my hands and tried to grab his wrists.

He was dunked then, pulled quickly, and then released.

"Mi...." Jake garbled my name, his mouth filling with water.

"NO!" I slapped the water with both hands. "NO! NOT HIM!" I swam closer to Jake. The Pit was wrong. It had it all wrong.

I tried to pull him, but he was so big. The Pit was wrapped around his ankle, or perhaps it had both legs by now. Jake went under again, his entire body trying to kick away to no avail. I could touch him still. I had my hands on his chest, and then he slipped further and I was holding his shoulders, then I pawed at his neck and finally I held his fingers. I pulled wildly, feeling myself go with him, sensing the water up my nose and in my eyes. For a single second I thought I would go with him, hanging on to his tightening grip, and be in The Pit.

I let go. I had to. I shuddered, the realization turning over in my stomach and my mind.

"nnnnoooNONONONO YOU STUPID FUCKING PIT!" I screeched at the night, at the now hushed water.

I could only hear my breath, ragged and desperate, as I tried to look down, tried to see the thing that had taken Jake. I had never seen it as a formed thing. Since I was a toddler I had sensed its closeness, its affinity for me, but I had never seen it. I had only felt it on my skin and heard it in my head. But I knew The Pit and I knew it was jealous. It was jealous I loved Jake. Knowing this somehow made me angrier. Fire rushed through my veins, it was a complete and overwhelming anger I had never known.

"I hate you, I hate you, I hate you," I cried into the water. I wanted to kill it. I wanted to strangle it and make it stop being.

It touched me then, swished by my ankles with a tender graze. I kicked at it and spat in the water. I could only whimper and shake. The cold night was overtaking me, making my teeth chatter.

I was alone. My thing had paddled away into the deep, leaving me to bob in the black water like an unanchored raft. It was with them. It was with them and not me. Shivering and tired, I swam back toward the shore. For one hopeful instant, when my toes touched the first particles of sand, I thought it was The Pit reaching out for me. No. I was more alone than I felt was even possible, and it wasn't Jake who I missed. I knew this fully. The Pit had abandoned me. My anger cooled and I could feel only an overwhelming loneliness.

"I'm sorry." My throat was raw from screaming. I wanted to say more, I wanted to reason with The Pit, make it understand it had made a mistake, but it was alright, I forgave it, I loved it. But I was in the shallow end, my butt in the sand, and it probably couldn't hear my words or my mind.

I cried. I didn't want to go back. I couldn't walk up to my apartment, dripping Pit water, and sleep. I couldn't work another shift, or play video games with my baby brother Dawson, or swim on a hot summer day ever again. There had to be a conclusion. I couldn't walk away from The Pit.

As though it heard my thoughts, it appeared. Perhaps it had heard me all along, where ever I was, every second of my life. I didn't have to be in the deep water as I had always imagined. This notion thrilled me. It rippled toward me, somehow blacker than the black water. It was the first time I had actually seen it. It was made of water and a void of lines or shapes. It created a powerful wave that pulled me forward, into the dark foamy water, away from the sandy shore.

And then The Pit twisted around my leg, harder than it ever had before. It did not feel loving like it had when I was a child. It did not caress me as it had after it had killed for me, but rather it squeezed with impossible strength. I knew this was what they all had felt in those last moments, all the ones I had made The Pit take for me. I was happy. I was happy to feel it come back to me, to want me. I was happy to know the unyielding command of my Pit.

I made no more sounds. My head went under and I knew I would breathe no more air. There was only blinding, infinite night. I was no longer cold or sad. As the slimy water rushed into my lungs, I was hopeful. Perhaps I couldn't go back to my life because I was going somewhere I was meant to be. A beautiful place The Pit created for us. We would be together and there would be no more jealousy. Where I was going there would be light. I wanted this to be true.

But as I descended, a creeping thought entered my last few moments of life. I was in pain all over my body and this made me wonder that if instead of my thing, the thing that loved me; it was actually Aiden Todd, no longer pale and freckled, but now a purple bloated slug that pulled me into the darkness. Perhaps Jake and his wife Andrea, still warm and angry were drawing me down. Maybe it was my Uncle Jeremy, slick with seaweed, a hollow skeleton in motorcycle boots, who clawed at my legs as I slipped down, further and further, into the murky, hungry maw of The Pit.

Meg Hafdahl

Hannah Goes Home

The double wide trailer was still a piece of shit. She knew this, though she had hoped for something more. There was a Spongebob Squarepants blanket stuffed into one of the narrow windows like a makeshift curtain, his maniacal grin taunting her. Her old bike, formerly purple, now a deep rusted red, rested against the metal side of the trailer as though she had just stepped off of it for a summer dinner of bologna and Kool-aid. There were roller skates and old ratty tires. There were tin cans and Chicken McNugget boxes. The trash, the piles of rotted things, looked wrong against the backdrop of the beautiful, clean woods. The trailer was a blight, a crime against the natural beauty of its surroundings.

Hannah couldn't bear to look. Not at the mess before her, the squalor she had climbed out of at age seventeen, or at the man next to her, taking it all in himself. Instead she looked down at her sweating palms and tried not to cry. But an escaped tear ran down her face and landed with a dramatic plop on her jean shorts.

"Hey," he squeezed her hand. "It's okay."

"It just, it looks even worse than before." Hannah found a tissue in the glove compartment and gave her nose a good wipe. "I'm just…you know. I'm embarrassed."

Her fiancé considered this as he stared at the crooked trailer. "I know. But you know you have nothing to be embarrassed about. You left here and you went to college and you did everything on your own, Hannah. You should feel proud."

Jason rubbed her shoulder, as he often did during his pep talks. He always saw the good in things, the positive side, and this was the first thing she had loved about him.

But he couldn't understand how truly horrible the trailer was. He couldn't know how her secrets were strewn about her childhood home just like the trash.

He opened his car door first. He was a foot taller than her and had the sort of wide chest and box chin that intimidated other men. This pleased Hannah, who herself was barely five feet and skinny as a rail. She was not skinny in the model definition, but rather awkwardly so.

Clothes hung from her bony shoulders and sagged under her scrawny butt.

She followed his lead and stepped out into the tall grass. The humid air was filled with mosquitos. They bred in the putrid creek down the hill. Hannah already had two red circular bites on each leg before she got to the tiny porch steps. Jason stood in front of her, subconsciously shielding her, she supposed, from all the nastiness.

He had grown up with two parents and a twin brother in the suburbs of St. Paul. He had hockey practice, birthday parties and trips to Disney World. His father sold insurance and his mother managed a small toy store. When he told her all of this over drinks on their first date, she actually trembled with jealousy.

Jason rapped on the door. She hovered behind him, desperately praying that no one would answer. Then they could run away, back to the hotel, and order room service and get naked. That would be much better.

But her older brother swung the door open and a cloud of cigarette smoke and body odor greeted them both. He looked at Jason with shifty, paranoid eyes. Greg was at least two hundred pounds heavier than the last time she'd seen him. His shirt, Spongebob again, tautly stretched over his hairy belly. His sweatpants were strained too, leaving a good amount of flesh exposed bellow his bellybutton. Hannah felt the blood drain from her face. Greg had once been her best friend, her only friend. But he chose to rot here. She had always known he would, but it didn't make the sight of it any easier.

"Hannah!" He smiled. The smile made it all worse. She could see the ghost of the boy he was, the skinny, awkward boy who only wanted to please their mother.

She forced a smile in return and wedged herself onto the porch with Jason. She hugged her smelly brother.

"This is my fiancé Jason," she said as she let go of his enormous arms.

Jason extended a hand. Greg took it within his chubby fingers, shaking vigorously.

"Mom says you're a dentist or some such thing," Greg moved out of the door frame so they could come inside. "We haven't seen Hannah in almost ten years."

"Yeah, I'm an orthodontist." Jason followed him into the trailer.

Hannah entered slowly, feeling at any moment she may scream. There was the familiar cacophony of fans blowing, the TV blasting and the smell of Vick's Vapo-rub. *Always that smell.*

"And, well, I'm glad we can come visit now at least," Jason said, surveying the living room. It was just as Hannah had warned him, filled with pointless things. The dishes were piled high in the galley kitchen and each place to sit was covered in random clothes and bags.

Greg pushed some of it onto the floor, huffing with effort as he did. He plopped down into a glider chair. "Mom's on her way home I'm sure. She was getting us some lunch, something special since you're here."

Just as Hannah took a tentative seat on the edge of the tattered couch, her mother's sputtering VW Bug sounded in the gravel pit they called a driveway. Her mouth was instantly dry at the prospect of seeing her mother, and simply from being in her mother's sphere of influence. She could sense the old feelings; the dirty churn in her stomach, and the immediate need to defend, to deflect.

Sandy busted through the trailer door with swinging Wal-Mart bags on each arm. Her spiky red hair, once a soft, natural orange, was now dyed blood red. She wore no makeup, she never had, but her face actually seemed a bit fresher than it had ten years ago. Her cheeks were flushed a youthful pink and the color under her eyes was not as black and haunted as they had been. She looked rather happy.

Jason took the bags from Sandy as he introduced himself.

"Ah! You are handsome!" She flapped her bare arms and then hugged him tightly. A limp cigarette hung from her lips. "How'd you ever get ahold of this one?" She looked over Jason's shoulder at her daughter.

"Oh, you know…" Hannah trailed off. She stood awkwardly and gave her mother a side hug. Sandy insisted on holding onto Hannah, pinching her side with curious hands.

"Look at you, you're damn skinny now girl." Sandy flashed her yellow teeth.

Greg sat back in the glider, watching it all unfold. He had a Fruit Roll-up he had produced from some hidden spot of trash and was winding it around his chubby finger.

Jason tried to place the bags on the kitchen counter, but they began to slip on a pile of dirty plastic cups.

Sandy snatched them back. "Just sit down you, I'll get it all ready."

She pulled out a cooked BBQ chicken, the type in a plastic case. There was a container of mashed potatoes and two small cups of coleslaw.

Jason obeyed and sat back down with Hannah on the couch. He rubbed his fiancé's back. "Okay?"

Hannah nodded.

"Where do you live now?" Greg licked his Fruit Roll-up wrapped finger. Hannah remembered doing that, twenty years ago, sitting on the small porch with Greg. It made her sick to watch it now.

Jason sat forward. "We live in an apartment right in downtown Minneapolis. We love it, we can walk to work."

"Oh." Greg licked. "We can't walk anywhere. It takes ten minutes just to drive to town."

"Yes, we're staying in Forsyth actually. I've never been to this part of Montana before, I'd just been to Yellowstone, as a kid," Jason said. Hannah found it both adorable and admirable that he was trying.

Clearly she could not have prepared him for the smell or the squalor that she had grown up in. But he rolled with it. He didn't sneer like the children had.

Sandy appeared with the first dripping paper plate. She handed it to Greg who poked at it excitedly with his stained orange finger. "Did I hear you live together?" She handed Jason and Hannah their lunch before tossing her cigarette into an overflowing ash tray on the coffee table.

"Yes Mom." Hannah could feel the walls within her rising. She didn't want to fight. She didn't want to feel the way she always had, as a severe disappointment and burden to her mother. This woman with a pathological need to date only assholes. This woman who couldn't bother to sweep or brush her teeth, but who found Hannah intrinsically disappointing.

The chicken tasted like dirt in her mouth. She couldn't imagine ever enjoying anything in that trailer. Not with that damn Vapo-rub smell stinging her nostrils.

"We work together too, but I guess Hannah's told you that." Jason took a considerable bite of potatoes. He hated mashed potatoes. Hannah smiled.

Sandy sat in the last available spot and lit another cigarette. She never ate with others. She had always treated food like a dirty secret, saving it for late at night when Greg and Hannah were asleep in their bunks. When she was older and could see the world more clearly, Hannah guessed it was because there was barely anything to eat, so her mother would sacrifice for her and Greg. But the thought of her mother going hungry just didn't fit into what she knew of Sandy. She was inherently selfish.

"At the clinic, yes. Hannah's really made something of herself. And now she's marrying you. It's hard to believe really." A curl of smoke blew into Hannah's face. The fans circulated the pungent air. There was never any fresh burst, just staleness.

"Oh I don't think it's hard to believe," Jason stiffened. "She's the smartest person I've ever known, and the hardest working."

"Hmmm." Sandy took a dramatic puff.

Greg balanced his plate on his belly. "Remember you said you were going to work at Riggs? Growing up you wanted to work there!"

"What's Riggs?" Jason put a protective hand on Hannah's knee. She sensed he could feel her mother's wrath, not just a concept anymore, but a real thing, focused in their direction.

"It's the funeral home." Sandy adjusted the waistband of her khaki shorts. "This girl was a morbid one." Greg giggled. Her mother stared at Hannah. She wanted to tell on her. She wanted to make her lose Jason. Hannah knew this.

Jason laughed. "You wanted to be an undertaker?"

Hannah shrugged. She had tried to forget that. She had tried to forget a lot.

~

She sucked in the summer air as though she had never breathed before. It felt so good to be outside, to be blinded by the setting sun. Jason held her hand as they returned to the car. Greg watched them from his bedroom window, the SpongeBob blanket pushed aside, so he could get a better view.

"I need a drink." Hannah waited as Jason opened her car door. He managed a crooked smile.

They drove down the gravel road until they met the paved street that led back to town. The turn signal clicked. Hannah was surprised by more tears.

Jason put the car in park and kissed her blonde head. "I'm sorry," Hannah whispered through the tears. "I'm sorry that's my family."

"Stop!" Jason unbuckled so he could wrap his arms around her. "It doesn't matter Hannah. Stop it. It's not that bad."

She turned, looking at the man she loved, a good man. "I lived in that shitty trailer." She wiped her wet face with the back of her hand. "And it smelled just like that, Jason, I can't do this."

He shook his head. His blue eyes filled with tears. In four years she had never seen him cry. Even when his cat died she had seen just a tremble in his lip. Now, a tear threatened to crawl down his face. This made her stop and watch him. He could see her pain, feel it.

"You can do this. You already did. We're going to take them to dinner tomorrow and that's it. We don't have to go back in there, okay?"

She nodded vigorously, thankful for him. But she couldn't help the feeling that she didn't deserve him. The idea burned in her mind, constant and aching.

~

They stayed in bed. There was nothing in Forsyth to actually do, and more than that Hannah was not interested in any more memories. She didn't want to go to the school or the river where she and Greg threw rocks and smoked.

They ate gas station food under the covers and watched bad TV. Jason played games on his iPad and she read.

She was thankful her mother wanted to eat at a new place, a Chinese buffet, rather than somewhere she would have to see and smell from her childhood. They would sleep one more night and leave forever. She knew this was it. There would be no visits once they had children. Her mother would never leave Montana, not even for her daughter's wedding. This, at least, was comforting.

The yellow VW pulled up ten minutes late. Hannah was hugging herself tight. She was in a striped sundress and suddenly her exposed arms and legs made her feel naked. The main street of Forsyth made her even more uncomfortable. The buildings and hanging flowers were just like before. Yet Jason was there, incongruous in her ugly childhood home.

Greg popped out first, surprisingly spry for such an obese man. His childlike grin was plastered on and he wore what looked to be the same, strained sweatpants along with a huge, flapping orange t-shirt. Hannah gave him a quick hug, aware of his body odor and sweating flab. How could her big brother be in there? That boy who kissed her head when she cried, who came home with stolen packages of sanitary pads stuffed in his waistband for her.

Sandy, in faded jeans and sparkly flip-flops, led them into the buffet. Hannah was grateful it smelled of wontons and egg drop soup, scents she didn't associate with her childhood or Montana. Now she just prayed there would be no familiar faces.

They settled in a booth and ordered sodas. Greg anxiously approached the buffet with an empty plate. He looked overwhelmed. Sandy talked as she piled her food. She asked Jason about his parents and his job. Jason acquiesced, answering each question slowly. Hannah thought he must feel pulled in a million directions. He felt a need to be polite to Sandy, even try to build a relationship with her, yet he instinctively must have hated her for hurting Hannah. This paradox made her heart ache.

"Hannah's thinking of going back to school, so she can move up from assistant to partner at my practice," Jason squeezed into the booth next to Sandy. Greg was still lingering in the buffet line.

"You're going to be an orthodontist then?" Sandy chewed on an egg roll. Hannah couldn't stop watching her mother's nicotine stained fingernails. They mesmerized her, they made her remember things.

"Hmm?" Hannah swallowed.

"I was saying you're going back to school." Jason looked as though he regretted sitting next to Sandy. He wanted to pat Hannah's knee or rub her back to assure her it would all be over soon.

"Oh yeah." She felt herself slumping down in the seat. She didn't have the energy to hold her shoulders up any longer, to pretend she was okay.

Greg slid into the booth next to her, filling all available space. She was beginning to feel trapped. The air of the restaurant reminded her of the stale trailer. She gulped her Diet Coke.

Her mother watched. Her eyes, always derisive, pinged from Jason to Hannah. She was going to say something. Hannah knew it would be something mocking and mean. She could predict this in her mother. As a child she knew.

"You live together you said?" Sandy wiped her lips with a napkin.

Hannah fumed. "You can't say much about that, Mom." Sandy had paraded at least ten different men through the trailer during Hannah's childhood. None of them gainfully employed or sober.

"No, it's just…." Sandy trailed off.

"What?" Hannah clenched her fork. She had no intention of eating the food, but she had to hold onto something.

Sandy carefully set the napkin on her plate, as though preparing herself for an important speech. "He must know then."

"Know?" Jason abandoned his chicken wing.

"What are you talking about?" Hannah felt a pang of fear, somewhere deep and black. Sandy raised her chin and tilted her shoulders, like she had a real, juicy secret to share. "What Mom?" Hannah repeated.

"He must know by now what you do, dear." Those yellow teeth revealed themselves.

Something long dead stirred within her. A memory, a haziness, an almost.

"I guess I don't know what you mean exactly." Jason laughed awkwardly, as though he had missed an old family joke.

Greg ate heartily, seemingly unaware of the tension rising around him.

"Oh well, it's not really my place to say," Sandy tapped a yellow nail on her glass. "But you do need to tell him dear. If not then I guess I'll have to."

Hannah couldn't breathe. She pushed at her brother's enormous thigh with both hands. He stopped, mid bite, and realized she was trying to get out.

Greg scooted out of the seat, a greasy napkin he was using as a bib fell to the floor. Hannah felt her throat closing up. There was no air.

She zipped past the buffet line and out past the register and tinkling koi pond. She was vaguely aware Jason was behind her, asking her what was the matter, was she sick?

Hannah sucked in the fresh air. The yellow nails and the yellow teeth and almost that smell, almost. She coughed and felt the welcome air in her lungs. She could control it, she could breathe and focus and control it.

Jason brushed his hands through her blonde hair as she bent over and regained her strength. He smelled of chicken wings and soap. He smelled good. She buried her face in his chest and cried hot tears on Main Street.

"What's she talking about Hannah? I'm missing something," he whispered into her hair.

"I don't know. I don't know." She shook her head, the tears wet on her cheeks.

"Then why are you so upset?" His curious eyes searched hers for an answer.

She clamped down her jaw. Breathe. Control it. "Take me back to the hotel."

Jason took a step back from her. "I'm going to pay, and I think I should say goodbye too."

"Fine." She sensed an unexpected iciness from deep within.

"Hannah," he put his hands in his shorts and looked down at the pavement. "If there's something from your childhood you haven't told me, something bad you did, or… you can tell me anything, I love you."

Something bad you did. She felt exposed. As though layers were being removed before she was ready. Before she could consent. Her mother had that power. Forsyth had that power. The thing, the dark thing, was coming, growing inside her. She could feel it, remember it, and predict it.

"I'm going." She tried to make it sound casual but her words came out all shaky.

"I'll meet you at the Super 8." Jason opened the door to the restaurant and disappeared inside.

Hannah pounded down the sidewalk in her designer wedges, keenly aware of the swish of the expensive dress on her legs. She couldn't go back to the hotel, not now, not when it – she – was coming and how could she have forgotten? How could she have thought she was free of it – her -- when clearly she never deserved to be?

Hannah rounded the corner of the dollar store and stopped in the alley next to a trash can and a pile of boxes.

Breathe Hannah. Breathe and control it. Maybe you can now. She was scared. Her mother was threatening her, squeezing her out. The light aura was coming, familiar and dreadful. And then finally the smell. Pungent and everywhere. The Vapo-Rub began to sting her nostrils. *Always that smell. Always.*

~

Time passed. She blinked hours away. Hannah found herself standing outside the trailer. She knew it, instantly, from the sound of the swaying branches scratching the metal sides. It was night and her legs ached. It made her think of a time before, when she woke, sitting in Mrs. Monroe's class with a gnawed pencil between her fingers. Her hands had throbbed.

She took a moment to take in her surroundings. The rural woods of Montana were dark as ink, just as they were when she was a child. She often wondered why her mother had plopped their trailer down in such a faraway spot. But, Hannah supposed, it had probably been for the best. At least her fellow school children didn't pass by her home every day, pointing and whispering.

She was unhappy to be back. Yet she expected it.

"Hannah!" Jason's voice cut through the starless night. "HANNAH!"

He ran to her. His handsome face was red and he was puffing loudly. "I've been looking everywhere, I didn't actually think…" He stopped. He stared at her sundress.

Although it was dark there was enough shimmering moonlight to see the blood. She was covered in it. And she was not surprised.

All the redness drained from his face. Hannah could see in the dim light that he instantly became pale.

"You're....you're hurt," he stuttered.

She shook her head. "Jason," she felt the stickiness on her hands but chose to ignore it. "Jason, have you ever seen a werewolf movie before? You know, like *Silver Bullet*, or the one in London?"

"What the, what the fuck are you talking about? Hannah, you're bleeding." He stumbled forward, reaching a hand out to her.

"Have you Jason?" Something cold and sharp was in her hands. She dropped it in the brown grass.

"Yeah, yeah," he cried. The threatening tear from earlier finally traveled down his cheek.

Hannah looked up at the half moon. "When I saw one, I don't remember which movie exactly, it was the first time I saw someone with my problem, with....with the same issue I've always had."

Jason trembled.

"I know they don't exist. Werewolves aren't real. I know that. It's just that in the movies they lose time like me. I lose time." She pulled her bloody hands to her body, hugging herself tightly.

She had practiced this conversation in her head a million times. She regretted waiting until now. She knew Jason could never forget her as she was in that moment, with warm blood dripping down into her cleavage. She regretted lying and making it worse. She should have done this years ago, on a bright Sunday morning at brunch. She was a coward.

His eyebrows knit together. She watched as he stepped backward. He was afraid. He was afraid of the trailer. He was afraid of the tacky blood down her front. He was afraid of her. The truth hurt Hannah. She held on to herself even tighter, just like she had as a girl, just as she had before time would run away from her.

Everyone around her took time for granted. Time was linear and predictable, something to rely on. But, just like every aspect of her childhood, time was defective for Hannah.

"Did you hurt someone?" Jason took another step away from her, from the trailer. He was confused. His eyes darted back and forth, as though planning a quick escape.

Hannah took in a deep breath. She didn't know how much longer she would have to explain. Now that she had lapsed, the first time in five years, she assumed there would be aftershocks.

The last time was in college. She looked down to start her biochemistry final and then came back, two days later, at the counter of a hardware store. Shaking and angry, she arrived back at her dorm to find someone had shoved something under her door. It was a copy of *Sybil*, an edition from the eighties.

For one awful second she had imagined it had been her mother. Her mother had found her and wanted to taunt her. Hannah huddled into a humid corner of her room for hours, opening to random pages in the book and reading lines. Finally she had flung it across the hardwood with a satisfying scrape. A few pages of *Sybil* made more sense to Hannah than all of the werewolf movies. This realization had burned through her like fire.

"I didn't hurt anyone." Now she wanted to fall to the grass. Her legs ached beneath her. She realized her wedges were gone and her bare feet were muddy and hot with pressure.

Jason walked to the side, giving Hannah a wide berth. He was trying to speak, his lips ghosted words, but no sounds came out. He moved forward and climbed the rickety porch. Hannah wanted to stop him from going inside. He didn't belong in that awful place.

"Jason!" She turned in time to watch him disappear inside. She had the oddest sensation she needed her mother, that she needed Greg. That they could help her somehow.

As she followed, she heard Jason exclaim in horror. It wasn't a scream exactly, more of a disappointed groan. She hobbled up the steps, her feet were beginning to feel numb.

There was blood on the couch and the glider chair. There was blood on the rust orange carpet and splatters of it on an errant bag of trash. Sandy was on her back in the deepest pool of it. She was wheezing for air, her hands clutched over a wound on her chest.

Hannah had never seen so much gore. She felt faint.

"CALL 911!" Jason fumbled into his shorts and found his phone. He tossed it to Hannah, but she didn't catch it. It fell to the floor with a soft thud.

"No!" Sandy coughed. "Don't!"

Hannah couldn't tell if her mother's head was soaked in blood or if it was just her vibrant hair color splayed on the floor.

"You're going to die." He pleaded with the woman on the floor. He was kneeling beside her, his fingers on her neck, searching for a pulse.

It seemed odd, Hannah thought, because she was clearly alive.

"Sit me up," Sandy croaked.

Jason shook his head. "No, no, we need an ambulance. Call them Hannah!" He pointed at his phone that had landed on a pile of dirty clothes.

"I said sit me up you twit!" Blood pulsed out of the wound and on to Sandy's hand.

Jason obeyed. He slid his hands behind her back and propped her up into his arms.

Sandy studied her daughter's face. She was looking for something, an indication of the other – her.

Hannah recognized this tentative look from her mother. It always came after the blackness. But then something more came across Sandy's pale features. She exhaled slowly and her face seemed to find rest and comfort. She looked almost young.

"Now get me a cigarette." Sandy motioned to her daughter. Hannah wavered in the doorway. "Now!" Her voice was wet and foreign.

Hannah jumped forward and got a fresh cigarette from a pack on the coffee table. She lit it with a shaky hand. There was drying blood under her fingernails. She placed the cigarette between her mother's blue lips.

"Don't call anyone," Sandy repeated. Her eyes closed as she took a long drag. Jason continued to hold her from behind.

Sandy coughed. A drip of blood ran out of her nose. "Greg'll help you bury me, back by the creek."

Hannah sunk to the floor next to them.

"If you call she's going to get in trouble. They're going to arrest her." Sandy sucked in another long drag. Hannah could hear a wheezing sound coming from the wound. Her lung was surely punctured.

Jason seemed to have lost the ability to form words. Instead he looked from Hannah and down to Sandy as though he were living through a terrible dream.

Sandy took a weak finger and fixed the placement of her cigarette. "Tell Greg to put me by the others. By Anson."

"No!" Hannah covered her face.

Sandy's face slipped even more, into a sort of relaxed acceptance. Her wrinkles were smoothed out and her eyes twinkled with a sort of understanding and happiness Hannah had never seen in her mother before.

"I deserve to be down there," Sandy panted. "I knew what Anson was doing, Hannah." Both of Sandy's arms began to shake. "I just wanted him to stop doing it to me."

"No….No, Mom…"

"He deserved to die like that. They all did. What she did, it was right. And I deserved this too. She should have done it a long time ago," Sandy whispered. "Bonnie was always stronger than you. *She* takes care of you."

Hannah sobbed.

"Bonnie said I was fucking everything up for you. And I always have." Sandy's head began to bob forward as though her chin was suddenly too heavy to hold. "It's true. She always could say the truth, even when it hurt. God I love her…."

Hannah had never heard her name before. Yet it oddly seemed natural, like Bonnie was an old friend she had briefly forgotten. More than that, she hadn't known, not really, what Bonnie had done to Anson, and perhaps a few more. But memories were coming, of waking wet with blood, of waking to Greg, digging. And the feeling of liberation, of a total and complete relief that she could go to bed at night and be truly alone.

Jason stared at Hannah. She watched as the realization of who Bonnie was found him. His expression fell and he seemed limp, worn out.

Blood trickled down Sandy's chin. The cigarette was stained red. She took one last, luxurious drag and then let it fall to her lap. Jason flicked it and Hannah snuffed it out with her heel. The burning sensation felt good. It reminded her she was in her own body, awake and alive.

Greg's booming snores reverberated down the littered hall. There was no smell of Vapo-Rub. She smelled only the iron scent of the blood, her mother's; the mother who left weak Hannah to fend for herself when the men came at night.

Hannah lost a whole summer once. When she came back, her mother had searched her face with eager eyes. When she realized it was Hannah, she was disappointed. Sandy's eyelids had drooped and her smile had slipped into a frown. She was sad to see Bonnie go. Bonnie was the strong one, the one she loved more.

Now, Jason let Hannah's dead mother out of his arms. He was bloody, panting and scared.

"Hannah," he managed. "We need help. You need help."

Hannah looked down at her sundress, red and crusting.

She wanted to crawl to him. She wanted to pat his shoulder and reassure him. She wanted to tell him Bonnie was done, she wasn't coming back. But Hannah knew this would be disingenuous. Hannah couldn't control *her*, as hard as she tried. Bonnie was a force stronger than Hannah.

Her mother was right. She was the weak one. She couldn't handle what needed to be done. The truth was maybe Hannah was more like her mother than she could ever admit. Because she too loved Bonnie, and, more than that, she needed her desperately.

No. Hannah shook her head. No, she had gone years without Bonnie coiling within. She had lived a life, a full life without her protector.

Hannah needed help. That was all. A little help, a real help, not the kind Bonnie provided. She stood above her dead mother and the man she loved, feeling an odd mixture of strength and acceptance. She would need to go somewhere for a while, a place with muted colors and hushed whispers. A place she had once feared, but now was grateful for. She raised her hand at the light and recognized that the dawn of a new morning trickled into the dusty, squalid trailer of her youth.

There's Something About Birds

There's something about birds. How they can just flap up into your face with those crepe like feathers and razor claws. And they're everywhere, behind you, above you. I don't know, maybe it's because they're sort of dinosaurs or maybe it's Hitchcock's fault, but they scare the shit out of me.

When I sense one close I can actually feel my shoulders going up to protect my neck. The thought of a bird, of its stinking, breathy beak needling the back of my neck, makes me want to curl up my body like a roly-poly.

So, when I saw the crow sitting on my windowsill, cocking her head to the side like she thought she was cute, I screamed.

I was too scared to slam the door of my bedroom shut. I thought about it. I even heard the door slamming in my mind. But instead I tripped into the hall and pressed my back against the linen closet. Thinking about turning around, of exposing my back to it, made my insides hurt.

"You little shit!" My shoulders were as high as they could go, pressing into my earlobes.

"Caw," the crow said. She turned her head to the other side and watched me with those beady, black eyes that invade my nightmares.

I thought about killing it. Her. It was a mother bird, I could tell by her superior air. And if she came toward me, wings extended and razor beak pointed in my direction, I probably would kill her with my own bare hands. No, no that's not true. I would scream and flail and cry and bleed.

She stayed on the sill, her black feathers pressed down on her body. The screen was ragged behind her. A hole had been chewed or scratched right in the center. Had the bird done it? Was it possible?

The thought of her, tearing through the mesh like that while I was safely in my bathtub, made me feel a sense of violation I had never known.

I realized I was wearing just a dingy yellow towel, tucked into a loose knot over my breasts. My wet, newly blonde hair slapped at my chin. I wondered if the thick strands looked like juicy worms.

"Caw....Caw," she said, as though she made perfect sense.

For the first time in months I wished for Carter. He probably wouldn't kill her, but he would be brave enough to shove her back through the hole she had made in the screen.

Men can sometimes be, in their own simple way, necessary. I stood there, my entire body a vulnerable live wire, watching my new housemate hop along the windowsill. Chipped paint twisted underneath her talons.

I wished for my old bedroom. The one in the suburbs with the view of the Carrey's hot tub and the backside of the elementary. It was a prison by the end, that room, that view. But I was sure there were no crows inside there now, perched on what was once my dresser or the end of our sleigh bed.

"Caw," she said once more.

I shuffled to the side, keeping my back against the wall. I forced myself not to blink. She watched.

As I moved down the hall, toward the narrow slash of stairs, I heard a ruffle of feathers. I couldn't see her anymore. But she was clearly moving, gliding with ease around my current bedroom, which consisted of a mattress, a threadbare quilt and a pile of paperbacks. If she ate through my only blanket, I would weep.

But more frightening than her ruining my possessions was the sight of her ebony head peeking around the open doorway and locating me with her eyes.

She huffed through her nostrils and splayed out her left wing as though she were pointing at me. I slowly walked backward down the creaky stairs, keenly aware of my complete nakedness. I struggled to cover my bare butt with the towel as I felt for the last two steps. I managed to keep my eyes on her as she hopped forward. Water dripped from my hair down my back.

She appeared on the landing, her strange toes curled on the top step. Both wings spread fully. There is something about their feathers, weird and veiny and scratchy. They are unknown yet familiar, stuffed in pillows, strung to make boas, commonplace but ultimately foreign.

I tried to rush, but I had lost count of the steps. There was one more than I had expected and my feet came down so hard I tripped backward onto my butt. My towel flung open as I landed on the wooden planks.

I had been alone so long I had grown almost comfortable with my own nakedness. I had no mirrors to remind me of my increasing age, to shed light on my stretch marks and wrinkles and hairy armpits. But I scrambled to cover myself with the bleach stained towel.

I didn't want her looking at me. But she was looking at me.

She hopped from the landing to the top step, wings still extended. I thought maybe she was injured, I had never seen a bird move so jerkily. But no. Although she could easily fly and be snacking on my hair or eating a hole through my stomach in seconds, she wanted to hop.

Her menacing face was all pointed angles.I knotted the towel around my body and jumped to my feet. I kept my eyes on my avian house guest as I backed up into the cramped kitchen. The back kitchen door was across the room and I briefly thought of loosening the rusty deadbolt but the thought of trying to work the bent metal while the bird lurked behind me was too much. So I scooted along the wall, around the unplugged, olive green refrigerator, my eyes searching the long stretch of the L-shaped counter.

Sun streamed through the thin curtains above the sink. The smell of my breakfast, fried eggs ironically, wafted through the small home. Her feet clacked and scratched at each stair.

There would be a knife, a pan, something I could scare her with.

I scuttled backward until I hit the small end of the counter with my hip. I lunged forward for the silverware drawer, to the left of the sink, searching for something useful. I was strangely aware of my exposed neck. My mind was oddly vacant. I could only sense the instinct to run, to hide, and to protect my feeble existence.

Something peeped before me, right above where my hands lingered at the drawer. A high trilling sound made my naked back crawl with disgust. I drew my hands back.

I hadn't seen them until they were right under my nose. There were two chickadees sitting on the counter. They were identical. Fat, fuzzy little things with sandy brown bellies and black foreheads. One snacked on an insect with its circular orange beak. I wondered where it had found such a juicy bug. The notion it had brought it inside my home made my stomach lurch.

The other chickadee shifted his head in a hundred different angles, the way only birds can. He caught sight of me and stared, just like the crow, but with tiny, pin head eyes.

They remained right above the drawer, the one full of plastic forks and a few knives. I imagined grabbing for the handle and them alighting on two of my fingers. I imagined the crunch of my skin and bones in their tiny but powerful beaks.

My logical side, the piece of me I had trained to keep quiet for a while now, struggled within. They were just birds, harmless little puffs. Some people even put feeders out to watch little chickadees in their backyard.

But they watched me, here, inside my pathetic home. Even the one with the bug juice running down its chin. Something pecked at the back kitchen door. It was a steady thrum, like a heartbeat, so hard on the wood it made the door tremble.

The chickadees danced to the edge of the counter on their tiny feet, expectant somehow. Something flapped inside my cooler, a big chest type full of ice and stocked with milk and cheese. The lid raised a single inch, revealing a flash of greyish green feathers inside.

I fell backward and felt the counter behind me. I shuffled down to the edge and then planted myself against the soothing reassurance of the wall. I clawed my fingers into the soft wallpaper, wishing desperately that I would wake from this dream.

The crow walked into the kitchen on clicking talons, her wings still outstretched as though she were a peacock displaying his colors. But all I could see in her entire being was black; deep, entrancing, bottomless black that swirled into nothingness.

The old back door began to split in the middle from the rhythmic pecking. The wood splintered outward, creating a pile on the floor. A black beak, larger and sharper than the crow's, worked through the narrow hole.

I scratched at the floral wallpaper, feeling my nails give way and splinter much like the door. I couldn't turn; I couldn't look away and let them get behind me. I would rather they pierced my eyeballs with the tips of their beaks than feel a whisper of them on my neck.

Something hit the window over the sink with a reverberating bang. My head pressed against the wall as tightly as possible. I could see the glass cracking underneath the curtain as well as a shadowy outline of a triangular head and feathery wings.

The bird, or birds, caught inside the cooler screeched and struggled. The chickadees hopped excitedly to the edge of the ceramic sink. Another one, a new one, popped out of the drain. I could see its black head and then its white chest as it pulled itself from the hole. Another followed, and another. The sink filled with Chickadees. They stood on each other. Some pulled playfully at their friends' feathers. Others chewed on plump worms that hung lifelessly from their beaks. Then they all stared.

Hot blood burned my fingertips as I scratched deeper into the drywall. The thing with the black beak managed to squeeze through the tight hole in the door and land with a soft thump on the floor. I watched as it stood on steady feet; majestic yet murderous. It was big. It looked like the crow, but its tail feathers were thicker and its beak curved more at the top.

"Nevermore," I feverishly whispered to my raven guest. I was going to die.

The crow, perhaps emboldened by the new arrival, leapt toward me. I shrunk toward the wall, as much as I could. It hopped toward my bare foot. I creaked my head forward to watch.

The sink was a sea of chirruping, fluffy birds, beginning to overflow onto the counter and the floor. The crow slapped her wings back down as she approached my toes. I wanted to slide my foot back, but I was afraid to make any sort of sudden movement.

She bent her angled head down and pecked at my big toe. The surprise and the pain fused together into a penetrating realization. I was awake. I was going to be pecked to death.

Another irony of course, because I had run away, like the coward that I am, from the prospect of being pecked to death. I was in this hovel, alone, because I couldn't take anymore pecks.

PeckPeckPeckPeckPeckPeckPeckPeckPeck

I couldn't kick her away because the thought of touching her with my skin was more repulsive than death. My fingers unhinged from their bloody grip on the wall. I wanted to grab at my toe, not bleeding now, but bruising quite quickly. I stopped myself from leaning over and exposing my back.

Her proximity made my flesh erupt in goosebumps. I tripped forward, continuing to press my shoulders up into my neck. She stepped back, allowing me to move across the kitchen, over a forming pile of chattering Chickadees, and into the front hall.

The raven blinked at me as I left the kitchen. I stepped past the staircase and into the front entryway. I wrenched open the front door and stumbled out onto the porch. I ran down the few steps, feeling completely vulnerable and naked.

My fingers were sore, my ankle cracked, and I knew if I felt the slightest breeze on the back of my neck, I would fall into the overgrown grass and die.

This was the first time I was outside without my enormous, obscuring sunglasses. I ran to the side of the house and began furiously removing the large, leaved tree branches concealing my car. I slipped off the camouflage tarp and threw it behind me.

Birds began to spill out of every conceivable entry to the secluded house. Cardinals, with their bright red-orange feathers and angry, dark eyebrows, emerged from the chimney in a drove. Seagulls squawked as they soared in a flash of white from the cellar. The raven hopped out of the front door, pointing as the crow had, with a single wing.

The keys were under the VW bug's driver seat. I slammed the car door, holding one hand over my ear as I started the car with the other. I turned the radio on full blast, but I could still hear their hellish noises over "Folsom Prison Blues." I peeled out onto the gravel road and didn't look back.

~

Lucky Liquor didn't open until eleven. I sat in the parking lot, still shaking while I counted an envelope of dwindling cash tucked inside my glove compartment. Cars putted by on the back street. A 'V' formation of birds flew overhead and I shielded my face, but they seemed uninterested in my hiding spot.

I was still only wearing a towel, which was admittedly a problem, especially since I needed to keep a low profile. I had a plan to ask a man, one going in to Lucky's, to buy me a cheap bottle of wine or maybe a six-pack of beer, I wasn't quite sure yet.

A man would definitely do it. My entire body still trembled. I licked at my bloody nails, ripping one ragged one off with my teeth.

"I'll get something to drink," I assured my shaking legs. "And then I'll go back and they will be gone."

I sensed rain. The air was humid and expectant. The sun began to hide behind hazy grey clouds. Then a scratching on the roof of my car, a skittering. My breath caught in my throat. My entire body was immobilized, my neck crawled.

She flew down onto the brown hood. Her accusing, spherical eyes glared through the windshield at me.

"Caw." She stretched out her wings. In one fluid motion she leapt at the glass and hit it with her powerful beak. An explosion of glass hit my face and lap.

How?

She pounced into the passenger seat. Her wings made a nauseating sound as they settled into the upholstery.

"Caw." She calmly rolled a few ball shaped pieces of glass with her beak onto the floor mat.

I could feel sprinkles of the windshield in my hair. But I could only think of my neck, of her biting my neck. I brushed some off my towel. Rain sprinkled in through the gaping hole.

"I can't go where you want me to. I can't. And I won't," I told her.

She considered this. Her head tilted from side to side. She flitted up onto the console between us and balanced on one foot. She used the other to scratch my upper arm.

I screamed and threw my hands up to my neck. If she reached up there, I would vomit from fear. She returned to the passenger seat gracefully.

"I can't I can't do it anymore, I can't face it anymore. You don't understand," I told the bird. "They, they, they….they pick at me. I can't. I can't. Don't you see? They take and they take and they take and they keep doing it until I can't breathe."

It's like a flapping bird on your neck, pecking at your vulnerable parts. She wheezed loudly through the strange holes on her beak.

"Caw."

I felt for the keys, they swung from the ignition. The scratch on my arm bled onto my terrycloth towel. Windswept rain spattered onto her wings, but she didn't seem to care. She watched me. I started the car, resigned. Yes, I had run away. But there was no running from her. She settled back into the seat, her seat now, ready for a ride.

~

We stayed on the back roads because of the broken windshield. If I tried to go over forty miles an hour, the wind would become too much and my towel would split open and my eyes would fill with dust. I had a great fear of a cop pulling us over. I worried what he would do to a naked woman with a crow in the passenger seat, but I also worried what the crow would do to him. A cop would surely recognize my face too, even with my bad blonde dye job.

We drove all day, winding through edges of towns, past strip malls and golf courses. We passed dozens of suburban enclaves; the kind of subdivisions with stubby little trees and identical ultra- modern houses with neon green lawns and names like Whispering Valley and Pleasant Orchard.

She seemed content in her spot, watching the world go by. Her avian head would turn and tilt. I figured she must be bored in a car, something so beneath her, something so human and simple. She could fly. She could fly above it all. It was enviable really, her ability to leave everything below.

As the evening added another dark layer to the presently grey sky, I knew Richmond, Idaho was ahead. The shape of the river was changing beside us, widening into a lake and taking a familiar form. Fields of ripening fruit, battered old bridges and gravel roads were beginning to come into my view.

She preened beside me, using her beak to pick at something under her wing.

"Can you read my mind?" I asked.

She snorted at this.

My face and arms were cold from the onslaught of wind and rain. My cheeks felt numb and my knuckles ached on the steering wheel. We were almost there.

The anticipation tunneled through me. I wanted to think about hurting her. I wanted to create elaborate plans that involved crashing the car. But if I let these thoughts in for too long, if I really considered them, if I turned them over in my mind, she would know.

So I kept my foot on the gas, fighting the urge to muse about her death. I thought, instead, about my own death by a million cuts. She could scratch me all over, peck my eyes and nose and belly. I don't think I could stop her. My hands would turn to ash if I tried to touch her wings. The notion of it, the possibility of it, terrified me.

"Don't you think it's worse to go back now?" I had to speak loudly because the wind was picking up and thunder growled in the distance. "I think you have it all wrong. If I go back now, if I keep going, I'm going to ruin everything."

"Caw." She spread her wings suddenly.

Fear caught in my throat. A shadow seemed to tickle the back of my neck.

"I'm just saying, all I'm saying is that maybe we need to think about this!" I yelled. "Everyone is better off!"

Every feather on her body seemed to ruffle and puff out. She paced the seat, her talons catching on the upholstery.

I couldn't look at the road any longer. I pushed on the brake and put the car in park. We were on a residential street, dotted with houses and parks and memories.

I turned toward the crow. She was violently angry, her feathers vibrated and her beak clacked open and shut.

My shoulders went up instinctively.

She flew forward in one easy, elegant motion and bit my bottom lip. Her eyes looked straight into my own as she did it, black and alien and vengeful.

I cried out, but kept my hands down until she spun backward and landed in her seat. Then I touched my bloody lip. It was swelling instantly and I could taste the metal tang.

You bitch. I thought but didn't say.

Well talking it out was certainly not an option. So I pressed on the gas and we started down Sunnyvale Street. A flash of lightening electrified the sky.

My lip throbbed and my stomach was a mess of knots and terror. She settled back down on her tail feathers and continued her grooming once more.

I drove down a narrow alley. The rain was starting to obstruct my sight. It was getting in my eyes and soaking through me. My towel grew heavier on my body.

The house was the third one down, on the left. I turned off the headlights as we puttered behind. I killed the engine and stared through the stormy night at the place I had escaped.

She looked too. Most of the lights in the house were on, creating a mysterious glow in the backyard.

Bree's scooter was on its side in the middle of the grass. The sandbox had been filled. Wet buckets and shovels were swimming in the day's rain. Plastic chairs, ones I had never seen, were arranged on the back deck in a semicircle.

We got out of the car. My legs hurt from the car ride and for the first time I realized I needed both a strong drink and something to eat. She hopped through the open hole where the windshield used to be and onto the hood.

A child's silhouette crossed from the kitchen into the dining room. Sadness slowly drifted through me. Everything I had run away from was going to be right back on top of me. But worse.

They would see me and they would cry out. "Mom? Mom? Mom? Mom? Mom?" They would claw at me. I could picture them already. Five little faces. Ten grabbing hands. Ten wide, questioning eyes.

I walked through the yard, aware of the wet grass between my toes. I ran my tongue along my throbbing lip. The pain reminded me that I had no choice. That I was a coward.

The crow flew down onto the ground and snatched up a wiggling worm hiding beneath the swaying tire swing. She violently tore it apart and chewed on it; a threat, I'm sure, that I too could easily be crushed by her.

My towel, heavy from the rain, slipped. I tied it around my breasts even tighter, suddenly very aware of my nakedness and of my scabbed fingers. If the rain and thunder had held off, the Carrey's would be bobbing around in their hot tub, Tiki torches lit up on all sides. They would see me in my own backyard, the vanishing neighbor returned. Perhaps they would think I was a ghost.

A ghost and her crow friend, haunting my suburban home to catch a peek of my perfect husband and my perfect children. I think they are perfect. It's me who couldn't do it anymore. It was me who got in over her head, thinking I could raise them all, thinking I could take the never-ending assault of runny noses and seeping diapers and bedtime fights. It's odd when you realize you can't do something that so many millions of women did before you, easily and instinctively.

The night was beautiful. Lightening flashed over the roof and thunder rumbled; closer now. The rain smelled of the earth. She flitted up onto a porch rail. Her feathers remained dry. The rain slicked down her wings as though they were waterproof. She nodded her black head, encouraging me to walk forward. I did. Her razor sharp beak shone in the glow.

The raven appeared in the darkness. He sat atop the roof, curling his claws into a shingle. His profile loomed above me.

A collection of cardinals joined him, their bright feathers now murky in the strange light of the storm. They drifted next to the raven, all staring down at my pathetic form; a runaway mom in a dripping towel.

The odd little fluffs came next. I stopped and watched as what looked to be about fifty chickadees emitted a harmonious chirp as they landed on the tire swing in perfect synchronization.

I understood.

This was my last respite for a while, here in my backyard. The yard I thought I had wanted, full of toys and mess and children. I had mere seconds left of solitude. Maybe, if I was lucky, I would get in lots of trouble for disappearing and spend some time in jail. I had daydreamed about that prospect in my former life. I had thought how splendid it would be to have my own bed and my own stack of books and never have to cook. They feed you three meals a day in prison, cafeteria style.

I placed a hesitant foot on the first wood step. This was my last stop before reality would envelop me in an unwelcome embrace.

Carter was always so boring.

"Reality, that's what you can't handle. You never could..." that was my loving husband's diagnosis of me. "I thought it was cute at first, in a rebellious sort of way, how you made up crazy things so much you even fucking believed it. The way you added and embellished and lived in your fake world. Jesus, what an idiot I was, I really thought you'd stop, for the children..." He could never appreciate a good story.

So, you see, if the birds had been anything else I would have let death come. If they had been a group of vicious bears with fearsome teeth, I would have given up and let them puncture through my muscles. If Carter had found me in my hiding place and pushed a gun into my temple, if he demanded I come home and live in suburban reality, I would let the bullet tear through my brain.

But there is something about their crackling wings and shifting heads and piercing beaks. There is something about the way they flap behind you, out of sight but always there. There is something about them on my neck, chattering, flitting, hurting. There is something about their knowing, ancient eyes.

There's something about birds.

Dust

Bailey Reed's dead piano teacher crawled up the gravel incline toward her; no longer concerned with beats per measure or improper recital attire. Instead, the elderly Mrs. Deveraux was pale eyed and slobbering. She had no real purpose, just to inhabit the Earth in her death, somehow both innocent and deadly.

Bailey, eighteen years old but with the round baby cheeks and small hands of a much younger girl, stopped pushing her Safeway shopping cart to adjust the wool scarf pressed against her mouth and nose. It was hot; a scorching summer day with no clouds for cover, but the scarf was a necessary element for the post zombie life.

"Hi, Mrs. Deveraux!" She said through the thick, red wool. "I'm afraid to say I haven't been practicing lately," Bailey watched the dead woman pant with exertion. "But don't get mad."

Mrs. Deveraux barely acknowledged her former student. She tilted her rotting head toward the muffled sound and then simply crawled past Bailey on her green hands and shredded knees.

Bailey continued to push her new finds down the rural road toward home. She was looking forward to getting home and making lemonade with the yellow powder she had taken from Alicia Oliver's pantry. She was very thirsty.

Bailey had chosen the Gregg's Christmas Tree Farm for that day's shopping trip. The Gregg family turned out to be a rather illiterate bunch, so she was only able to find a family bible and a Betty Crocker cookbook. Both books bounced along in the cart, underneath a smattering of canned and boxed food, a package of paper napkins, and a plastic bag full of assorted batteries, two clean pillowcases, a stuffed bear with button eyes, and a box of matches.

The Pop-tarts didn't make the cart. She finished off the single package of the strawberry frosted ones she had found as she sat on the Gregg's front porch. Bailey watched Andy Gregg, fourteen years old and covered in swollen acne for eternity, walk shaky circles around his family farm. She thought, as she licked the pink filling from her cold Pop-tart, that every time Andy passed he seemed a little more sure footed, a little more purposeful in his walk. She pushed up her scarf and made sure it was around her face tightly before she walked past putrid Andy Gregg.

Bailey made it home and scooped up the books and the stuffed bear in her arms. She carried them upstairs to her bedroom and dropped them on her bed. She would organize her finds later, after lunch. She tore the scarf off and sucked in a few fresh breaths. It felt good to have the itchy thing off her skin.

"Dad!" She bounded back down to the kitchen. "Dad!"

He appeared from the cellar steps, a jar of homemade apricot jelly in his hands. Her father was only fifty, yet the deep lines of a troubled few years covered his forehead. His tired eyes completed the old, gray look. As much as Bailey looked younger than her eighteen years, her father looked older than his fifty.

"Dad we need to go back to the Gregg's. They have some containers with gas in their garage and the comfiest chair, like it's a recliner and brand new and really super cushy, like I almost fell asleep in it." Bailey took a knife from the drawer in preparation for lunch. "Oh and I grabbed some batteries and matches and stuff."

Her father nodded thoughtfully. "I think our chairs are just fine Bailey, we don't need to steal theirs."

"Steal!" Bailey huffed. "Andy Gregg spends his afternoons walking into the side of his dad's tool shed face first. I don't think he cares if we take his chair."

Bailey's dad lowered his shoulders and gave her a disapproving side glance as though she were sharing blasphemous gossip. "Get the graham crackers down."

She obeyed and they ate crackers and jelly in silence. She would just have to go back to the Gregg's on her own, take her dad's wheelbarrow or something and load the damn chair herself. Her father could be so infuriating. But he was the only human living in Ferris, Washington aside from Bailey. And she loved him, of course.

After their simple meal, Bailey's dad retired for a nap. She didn't know how he could sleep in such stuffy heat. There of course was no electricity to pump through the central air. They couldn't leave the windows open. The death dust could trickle in.

So she found her cat Mittens, adopted rather informally right after the dead began tripping around the planet, and fed her a tin of tuna from the Gregg's. Mittens was appreciative, as much as a feline can be, and rubbed against Bailey's leg. Bailey reveled in the tone of Mitten's rumbly purr. It was a pleasant sound. It didn't make her think of the guttural moans of the dead or of the disapproving tsks of her father.

After her visit with Mittens, Bailey decided to don her scarf once more and go out into the sunshine. She let Mittens out into the daylight to hunt for mice or laze in the heat. Bailey liked the feel of the heat on her skin too. She had missed the sun while her dad and she had lived in the cellar for all those months. She would never take the sun for granted. Or anything for that matter, anything at all.

She walked along her neighborhood in her frayed jean shorts and pink tank top. She wore a pair of sensible sneakers in case of broken glass or some other indefinable hazard her father worried about. The scarf was probably an over the top precaution, but it was the only way he would let her out on her own to do her shopping and exploring. Sometimes Bailey thought it would be enough just to have one of her dad's handkerchiefs tucked in her pocket for emergencies. But, she admitted, a scarf had come in handy when her dead high school friend Alicia Oliver sneezed death dust all over Bailey.

She had been reading Alicia's diary, a gripping and surprisingly dark read, when Alicia, missing both eyes and stumbling like a drunk, fell into her old bedroom and began hacking the powder up out of her chest. Bailey immediately pressed the scarf to her face and jumped over the dead cheerleader. She held her breath the entire run home. Her father made her burn her clothes and take three consecutive baths. He said the dust could still be on her, in her hair or under her fingernails.

Bailey continued walking down Willow Creek Road categorizing each empty house in her mind as either shopped or in need of shopping. She only liked to do one, maybe two places a day. She had to pace herself. Ferris wasn't a metropolis. The day would inevitably come when she had filled her cart with the books and the batteries and the trinkets of the last house. The thought of her purpose wilting away, leaving her alone, chilled her warm face.

A dead man paced the front yard of a split-level on the corner of Willow Creek and 10th Ave. Bailey watched as he tripped over a large, plastic candy cane. He lay on the ground, his face obscured by the overgrown grass. Most houses in Ferris still had their holiday lights strung and fake poinsettias sitting on their porches. Some had scraggily, dried up Christmas trees in the front window with a pool of fallen ornaments beneath.

The zombie finally got on his knees and rose up from the ground. He stepped over the fallen candy cane and stood still. Bailey crossed to the other side of the street as she adjusted her scarf. She could see pink slime smeared on the dead man's pale cheeks. He must have inhaled death dust. It made pink stuff come out of your mouth and nose in just a few short seconds. A lot of people choked and died that way.

The dead man, tall and perhaps in his early forties when he inhaled the dust, turned and watched Bailey with blank eyes. He kept his dead gaze on her as he reached into his front jeans pocket and removed a keychain. Bailey stopped mid step. Her foot wavered above the cement. Fear churned in her belly.

He turned, the keys dangling from his right hand, and marched up the few steps to the front door of the split-level. His back was to her, and the sunlight was irritating her eyes, yet she could tell what he was doing. Bailey placed both feet on the sidewalk and swallowed down the fear. It was impossible. He couldn't possibly be. He was dead. He was dead, rotting flesh like the others. But then she heard it, all the way from the other side of Willow Creek Road. She heard the punch of the deadbolt rotating, the jangle of the key chain returning to his dead hand and then the reverberating slam of the front door. The zombie had unlocked his front door and gone into his house as though he had just returned from a trip to the diner and not from Hell itself.

Bailey took in a deep, sweaty breath. She tasted a mix of the wool scarf and her own saliva. She turned and began to run back toward home, just as she had when Alicia Oliver had hacked dust everywhere. Bailey ran back toward her father.

She had noticed. She had noticed that the dead seemed to be attracted to their own homes and former haunts from when they were living. But she had never, never, seen one use a key or even complete the simplest of actions. They had just been merely vessels for the death dust, bumping around and spewing it out like mobile poisonous plants.

"DAD! DAD!" Bailey jumped the porch steps and skidded into the front hall. "DAAAD?"

Her father poked his head out from his bedroom at the top of the stairs. "Jesus Bailey, what is it? What happened?"

The concern in his eyebrows and the tousled nature of his graying hair somehow made Bailey feel at ease. Perhaps it was just knowing he was still there, that the earth hadn't shifted once again to reveal something more frightening then the dead digging out of their graves. Life was going forward; life had some predictability, like the expected messy bed hair her father displayed after every nap.

Bailey ripped the scarf from her face and tried to catch her breath in the scorching, humid house. Her father watched her struggle for air.

"Did one of them touch you? Or....or... or cough on you?" He didn't move from behind his bedroom door. "Did they get their dust on you Bailey?"

She shook her head. "No, God, it's just a million degrees!" Bailey swallowed hard. "But, Dad, I saw something, I saw one of them do something."

He slowly creaked down the stairs, the worry still etched into his brow. "What?"

"This zombie, this dead guy, he looked right at me and then, I swear, he got out keys from his pocket. Dad, he took the keys and actually used them. He actually put the key in the lock and got into a house down the street."

Her father blinked furiously. He was attempting to process what she said. But Bailey knew. She knew he was thinking of her mother, his wife. The pain flashed over his face in an instant.

"He could actually do it," she continued. "The zombie knew what a key was for. I think it was his house, like his house before he became a zombie."

They stood in their front hall, the only two non-dead residents of Ferris, Washington, and tried to make sense of it.

After a while he spoke, "No." He stared through her. "No, that can't be."

"Dad?" She took a step toward him but he put out his hands to stop her.

"No Bailey. You're wrong," he said it with such formality, with such confidence, that for a single second she actually believed him.

She opened her mouth to protest, but the pain in her father's eyes radiated with such intensity she had to stop. She stayed silent, watching him as he retreated back up the stairs. He would stay in his room for the rest of the day. Or maybe he wouldn't come out for a whole week. It was her fault.

He was acting just as he had in the spring when they were planting seeds in their backyard. Her father's boss at the credit union, Tom something, had come trudging up Willow Creek Road and her father actually believed he was alive.

Tom's left arm was nearly detached; it had dangled from his shoulder like a loose tooth. His eyes were white with death, but her dad ran toward him with arms open wide for a reunion. Bailey had to physically hold him back. She had to tell him, more than once, that Tom from work was dead. He would just flop around and get death dust on them. Her father slept for four days after that, leaving her in such a deafening silence that she would desperately press her face into Mitten's fuzzy belly, just to hear the purr, just to hear the heartbeat.

Now, her father left her in the front hall and walked back up the stairs. He slammed his bedroom door with an angry flourish. Just like the zombie down the street!

Bailey took a bottle of water and added the lemonade powder she took from Alicia Oliver's house. She sat on the front porch waiting for Mittens to return. She wanted to talk to her, to pet her and to feel less alone.

She thought of the zombie with the keys. What was he doing in his house? Was he walking in circles, stumbling over furniture and old Christmas presents? Was he pressing the remote with his purple hands, wondering when the damn channel would come on? She had shopped that house. She couldn't remember all she had taken, but Bailey was sure she had carted away a considerable cart full of books from that split level. She had taken blankets and a nice knit cap, perfect for the rainy Washington winters. Was he looking for his books? Was he searching for his knit cap, the one that was currently wedged into Bailey's overflowing dresser, to warm his lifeless head?

Mittens came back. Bailey squeezed the black cat until it finally escaped her grip and licked itself clean with its white mitten like paws. They sat together and watched the blazing sun sink into the horizon. Bailey didn't want to think of her mother, the thought of Mom made her father weak. It could only do the same for her. Yet the summer evening, buzzing with fireflies, forced the image of her mother into her mind.

Sondra Reed had sat on the very bench swing Bailey sat on now. She had been in the late stages of cancer then, a few weeks from death. Her skin was a sickly green and her bald head was wrapped in a flapping, silk scarf. She was in perpetual agony, but she didn't let that wipe the sincere smile from her gaunt face. She rocked back and forth in the swing, taking life in, enjoying it.

Bailey didn't want to remember her mother. Because remembering brought the thought, the fear, that Sondra Reed, librarian and avid snow globe collector, was working her way out of her grave over at Shady Forest Cemetery. The image of her mother, dead alive, digging through the dirt with her long fingernails haunted Bailey from the moment the dead woke. Sometimes she felt she was brave enough to check, to creep over to the cemetery and see if her mother's resting place was undisturbed. But she always chickened out. If she looked down into a gaping hole to see the busted open coffin, she would lose her mind.

"Let's go shopping." Bailey suggested to Mittens. She jumped off the porch quickly and grabbed onto one of the many empty shopping carts parked in her front lawn.

Mittens didn't want to sit in the cart, so Bailey opened the front door and let the cat inside the house. Her father was still behind his bedroom door. She would just go shopping alone, like always. She wouldn't take her scarf. It was too hot, even in the waning light, so she would just have to be careful and not get close to the dead.

She purposely steered her cart in the opposite direction down Willow Creek of the split-level with the key zombie inside.

Mrs. Deveraux's house was on 8th Avenue, a few blocks past Ferris Elementary and sandwiched between two houses Bailey had already shopped. She hadn't actively avoided her piano teacher's home; she had just been saving it for a down moment, a bad day. Bailey knew there was cupboard full of lollipops and caramels for good little piano players. Sometimes she would lay awake at night wondering, hoping, Mrs. Deveraux had done a decent grocery shop before the apocalypse. She had always been a prepared and organized woman.

The front door was unlocked. Bailey went straight to the cupboard, right next to the sooty piano, and was pleasantly surprised by the treats. She poured out cinnamon potpourri from a decorative basket on the coffee table and filled it with the candy. As she ran out to the cart and placed the basket inside, she noticed the light dying quicker than she had predicted. Perhaps they had passed the solstice now and it was late summer turning into fall. She wasn't really sure about days or even months anymore. Night was coming fast.

There were no dead milling about on 8th Avenue at least, the street was empty and quiet. The same complete quiet that deafened Bailey's ears and made her feel as though she were the last person on Earth.

She hurried back into the house and began to scour the kitchen. Mrs. Deveraux's back kitchen door had been haphazardly nailed with boards. Ironic, Bailey considered, since the front door had been unlocked. But most people had died right away, in the middle of it all, not knowing about the dust until it was too late. Everyone had thought the zombies were going to be like the ones in the movies, hungry for human brains. So they started shooting them in the head with hunting rifles and handguns, because that's what worked in those Romero films, but the reality was shooting them made the dust really fly.

Bailey found saltines and Cheerios and lots of herbal tea. She made a few trips to her cart with armfuls of food. As she was making one last pass in the kitchen, and considering what she would find upstairs, the wood floor creaked in the living room.

Life had become so silent now, so achingly quiet, that the sound of the wood floor underneath shifting weight sounded like a firecracker to Bailey. She dropped a handful of sharpened pencils on the linoleum and held her breath. It was instinct now to hold her breath and try not to breathe in the death dust.

She would have to lean forward to see through the doorway into the next room. Bailey wished she had the comfort of her scarf pressed against her lips. The scratch would be reassuring.

There was more creaking, definitely a dead one walking about, but they were moving with such hesitation it made Bailey worry, it made her very scared.

Then another sound, cacophonous in the vacuum of this new life, made Bailey actually hold her trembling hands over her ears. It was a sliding on hardwood, a long and deliberate pull of something. Bailey took in a few shallow breaths and then held her mouth closed again. She forced herself to lean forward and peek into the living room. She could see nothing, but a couch littered with pillows and the front door, gaping open. She tiptoed over the fallen pencils and as she took her first actual step into the doorway. A sound shot through her, so unexpected and jolting, that she screamed.

Her scream echoed endlessly in the silent neighborhood. "The piano." Bailey whispered to herself. Someone was pressing on the piano keys, slowly and purposely.

Bailey took off her tank top and wrapped it around her mouth and nose. She would just have to walk back home in her sports bra and shorts. It would be nice if her partial nudity would lure an interested, handsome stranger from a house or behind a fence, but she knew of course it was just her and the zombies. They probably wouldn't leer at her belly and breasts, although she wasn't so sure now.

Once she was certain her mouth and nose were covered properly she took a wide step into the living room. Mrs. Deveraux sat on the piano bench, her piano bench, playing the black and white keys like a curious toddler. The dead woman pressed her ear to the instrument. She turned her head from side to side as she tested each key. She likes it, dead Mrs. Deveraux likes the piano.

Bailey watched the performance unfold. She wasn't frightened by the proximity of her dead piano teacher. It was the thought of old Mrs. Deveraux crawling down eight street on her scratched up knees and useless legs, perhaps struggling all afternoon, so she could return to her beloved piano, that unsettled Bailey Reed.

Mrs. Deveraux didn't care about her visitor. She began to experiment with the keys, hitting different combinations with all the strength she had in her decaying fingers. With each tuneless strike Bailey thought of the living Mrs. Deveraux reminding her to curve her fingers and play softly. *Softly Bailey girl.*

"You'll need this." Bailey opened a filing cabinet and took out several manila folders. She removed an easy lesson, one for the kindergarteners, and carefully extended out her hand to put it on the piano.

Mrs. Deveraux huffed out her nose in response. Bailey jumped backward, aware of the dust. She watched Mrs. Deveraux, the tender old women who held Bailey as she cried over her dead mother, who was now a zombie with white bones poking out of her shins, take the paper and begin to look at it.

Look at it.

Bailey left. She walked out of the house, the piano clanging behind her, and saw her shopping cart full of caramels and knick-knacks. She walked past it.

She walked past Ferris Elementary where an unsmiling, lone zombie girl in a Christmas dress with white fur trim tried to slide down a twisty, purple slide. The dead girl skidded down jerkily and then climbed off to try again. Bailey walked down Peak Street and saw Mr. Oliver, Alicia's dead grandfather, sitting in his yellow VW Bug. She couldn't be sure it was him, he had blown his face off when the dust took Alicia, but she was fairly certain because he was sitting in the front seat and had hands on the wheel like he was driving. He loved that car.

Dairy Queen was open. Freddy Cowell, wearing his uniform until it would eventually fall off his dead form, had flipped the metal sign to indicate he was ready to serve. But, as Bailey watched him through the glass, he just stood behind the counter dead eyed and in the dark.

Dark. Bailey looked up at the night. The stars were beginning to reveal themselves.

She knew what she had to do. Her purpose pounded in her mind. She ran back to Mrs. Deveraux's and was actually pleased to hear the music still playing. She scooped up the basket of candy and ran back into the living room.

"I'm sorry!" Bailey said through the tank top plastered to her mouth. She poured the food back into the treat cupboard. "I'm sorry I took it."

Mrs. Deveraux didn't look up.

After she returned all of Mrs. Deveraux's belongings, Bailey took her cart and ran back home. Mittens meowed a greeting as Bailey ran up the stairs, two at a time, and began to fill her hands with her things.

She had stolen their things.

She had taken things from nearly every house and business in Ferris and now she would have to return it all. She would spend all night and the next week returning it all. It was her purpose, her reason. A tall stack of books wavered in her hands as she passed her father's room. His door was open and he was not inside.

"Dad?" Bailey had removed the pink tank top from her face and had put it back on, for her father's sake. She was now using her chin to balance all the stolen library books. "Dad?"

"Down here Bailey! You've got to come here! We're in the kitchen."

"Who? Who, Dad?" Her balance faltered and the books scattered down the stairs. She felt a cold impossible truth grip her stomach. "DAD! Who's in there with you?"

He didn't answer.

When Bailey entered the kitchen she first saw her father's bright smile, illuminated by one of the many battery powered lanterns she had stolen from her neighbors. His smile was wrong and misplaced. Next she saw he was sitting at the table holding her mother's hand. The zombie had her back to Bailey but her bald head, no longer wrapped in a silk scarf, was indeed her mother's. She was dirty from the grave, soiled, and, despite the costly embalming, she had spent the last few years decaying.

Her dead mother turned smoothly, like a human, and revealed her face. She had concave cheeks and rotting eye sockets. In fact, she had only one eyeball that looked as though it would roll away at any moment. Her nose was gone.

Bailey no longer felt galvanized about the things. As her palpable fear rose, her guilt over the Pop-tarts and the Sudoku books lessened. It wasn't stealing. She wasn't taking from people.

They weren't alive. No matter what they did, they could twist keys and play the piano, but they were still just lumps of flesh. Poisonous flesh.

"Don't touch her." Bailey felt the hot tears streaming down. They were big ones, like raindrops.

Her father simply shook his head. "Your mom's home, Bay, she's home."

"Mom died. Don't you remember Dad? She died." She couldn't see. The room, her parents, swam in the sea of her tears.

He didn't speak. He just pulled the flesh that once contained Sondra Reed closer for a hug.

The zombie obliged.

"THE DUST!" Bailey screeched. "She's going to cough soon, or sneeze, and the dust will kill you!"

Her father's eyes sparkled at the thought. She could see that. She could see the excitement in his face.

"They might get smarter." Bailey wiped her eyes. "They might walk to work and find their homes and use keys. But they are dead. Mom's not in there. Mom wouldn't come back here. She wouldn't bring the dust here."

The smell of her dead mother, rancid and strangely sweet, choked Bailey's throat. She put a hand over her mouth and took tiny, shallow breaths.

Her father continued to hug the dead body.

"They don't need things. They don't need food or books. I didn't steal." She began to back away. "They're just dust. They're dust."

As Bailey walked backward out of the kitchen she watched the last living man in Ferris Washington plant a chaste kiss on the paper thin cheek of her dead mother.

She knew he was weak. She knew he had lost his purpose a long time ago, even before the dead came. Bailey cried as she filled her cart. She didn't go back in the kitchen. She couldn't see his deluded eyes and more than that it would be full of dust soon. Instead she took the food stash from under her bed, the Bronte novels and the notebooks. She took batteries and knives and the stuffed bear from the Gregg's farm. She took quilts, clothes and a puzzle and matches. She took a flashlight and then finally she took Mittens. Mittens cozied into the quilt, ready for the adventure.

She would take everything. She would not feel bad. She would feel no guilt because the world was full of things, forgotten and abandoned, and she would breathe life into them. She would own them.

Bailey walked on in the dark, past the zombies plodding along the sidewalk looking for their homes, past the piano music still emanating from Mrs. Deveraux's, past the Dairy Queen with no Blizzards or banana splits.

She would push her cart until there was a human like her, a real one, with thoughts and feelings and a purpose. She would walk until there was a meadow of flowers and a bubbling stream. She would lay down in that meadow, with the other human and Mittens too by her side, and they would breath in the fresh air. There would be no more death and no more dust. They would see only the pollen of a new spring swirling through the vast and endless sky, searching for a place to grow and create life.

The Rainbow Inn

The Rainbow Inn would die without her. Freddie was certain of that. It was a dinosaur, an old-fashioned L-shaped motel built before she was even born, now destined to crumble into oblivion. It was in the far Northeast corner of El Paso, out past Fort Bliss and surrounded by the impossible, lonely desert. Once she was gone it would be gone too. But that was fine, because although her life was inextricably linked to the Rainbow, she hated her little motel.

It satisfied Freddie to think of it falling apart, rotting from inside out. Maybe if her dad hadn't given it to her she could have had a life, a real one with friends and maybe a lover and one of those secluded ranch homes in the mountains, up where the rich people live. Instead she had been pushed to the outskirts of town, out where people only drive past the Rainbow and squint in the Texas sunshine.

But more than her father's well intentioned gift of a motel, Freddie knew her looks had the most negative effect on her life. She was painfully ugly and her bitterness and sour nature had only made her features more pinched. Her face was a red circle, always flushed and sweating. Her large breasts swung low and heavy since puberty and her bulbous nose flared with every breath. She spent her sixty four years of life learning and accepting the limitations of an ugly woman.

Freddie sat at the Rainbow's front counter cataloguing her life's injustices. She watched Tilly arrive in her boyfriend's Honda. The eighteen year old swung her effortlessly beautiful blond hair and waved to her boyfriend. She then swung open the door to the Rainbow lobby with an unexpected enthusiasm.

"It's awfully early for smiles." Freddie nodded toward the dark morning sky. Pink light was just beginning to skim the quiet desert.

Tilly stopped and considered her boss. "I gotta show you this Fred." She pulled a folded paper from the pocket of her jean shorts. "I'm so excited!" She placed the paper in Freddie's chubby hands.

Freddie unfolded it carefully. The letters U.T.E.P were in bold dark print on the top.

> Ms. Matilda Forrest,
> We are pleased to inform you that you have been accepted to attend the University of Texas-El Paso in pursuit of your bachelor's degree...

Freddie didn't read anymore. She felt a bizarre hollowness in her belly. Her mouth felt dry. She handed the letter to beaming Tilly.

"Oh, well that's very nice," Freddie managed.

"The best part is that Sam got in too!" Tilly slipped the letter back in her pocket. "We're so happy, we're going to try to do a few classes together, you know like the required boring ones like Biology and stuff."

Freddie pushed out her lips. "Sam?"

Tilly began brewing the first pot of coffee for the guests. She looked over her shoulder. "Sam. You know Sam, my boyfriend."

"Isn't he Mexican?"

Tilly turned with the coffee scoop in her hand. She raised an eyebrow. "Whatdya mean Fred?"

Freddie could feel the red blazing on her face. "Well, I mean aren't there rules about that sort of thing? Them just coming and going to school here?"

Tilly rolled her eyes. "Sam's parents are from Mexico if that's what you mean. He was born in Alamogordo." She turned back to her task. "You better stop saying stuff like that, cause no one is going to put up with you when I'm gone."

"Gone?" Freddie leaned her considerable weight against the counter. She didn't feel well.

Tilly hesitated. She switched the coffee on and then finally said, "I'm going to stay on as long as I can. But my hours will have to change is all, to suit my school schedule."

Freddie was flooded with relief. She tried to regulate her breath quietly, but instead she took in a large, gulping gasp. Tilly pretended not to notice.

They got to work setting out the Rainbow's continental breakfast. This had been a new idea implemented by Tilly. She said people expected something more than shitty coffee. So now they had juice and yogurt in a glass bowl with ice, Danishes and donut holes.

Freddie helped herself to a cherry Danish and a handful of the donut holes. She liked this new change.

A man emerged from the door marked with the number eleven. Freddie remembered him from the night before. He had been alone and was rather quiet while she checked him in. She liked that he kept to himself because sometimes men liked to talk and joke and she felt they wanted to make her smile. She didn't want to smile. She thought maybe she had forgotten how.

The quiet man walked slowly into the separate lobby. He didn't look at Freddie or Tilly, which was more surprising. Instead he went straight for the coffee. His hand shook as he poured the hot liquid into a paper cup.

"Good Morning, Sir." Tilly was still indefatigably chipper this morning. She was in the far corner of the room preparing her maid cart.

The man didn't answer. Instead he slipped onto the ratty lobby couch. It had been there when Freddie's dad had purchased the place. It smelled of cigarette smoke and a dank cellar. Freddie never sat on it. The man stared straight ahead, through the floor to ceiling glass and out where the sunrise painted the desert with the colors of morning.

If Freddie hadn't spent her whole life in El Paso, waking early for crappy jobs her entire existence, she thought perhaps the sight of the orange sun rising over the desert would be beautiful to her.

But instead she watched her quiet customer. He was pale and his bangs stuck up comically, as though he had pulled his hands through his hair to purposefully create this odd effect. He, like Freddie, wasn't appreciating the beauty outside either. He held the coffee to his lips but didn't actually drink any.

The man mumbled incoherently. Only the paper cup was close enough to hear him. Freddie looked down and fiddled with some papers on the counter. It was going to be a strange day. She could feel the air in the tight lobby change. She would go on a short walk later, once the customers left their donut crumbs and soda cans for Tilly to pick up, once it was just the two of them again.

"There's something wrong." The man sat his cup down and was leaning forward, hands clenching his thighs.

Tilly responded first, "I'm sorry sir?"

He lurched forward putting his head between his knees like he was assuming the position of an ill-fated air passenger.

"Sir are you ill?" Tilly dropped a stack of wrapped soaps and rushed to the man.

He nodded weakly. Tilly retrieved a mop bucket and slipped it under his bowed head. He spit a few globs into the bucket and then vomited. The sour smell reached Freddie as the man continued to retch. The air in the lobby was rancid now, unlivable. She would have to go on a walk very soon. Freddie felt for the familiar bulge of the lighter in her slack's pocket.

"Oh my I hope you didn't eat at Perrito's down on Industrial. This happened to me when I had their taco platter." Tilly flitted around the sick man.

He sat up, wiping away the pink vomit on his chin with his flannel sleeve. "No, no there's something wrong with the room."

Tilly looked at her boss. Freddie shrugged.

"There's something bad in there, something sick." His voice was thick and shaking. Tilly and Freddie exchanged another look. "And the worst part is the scratching." He stared straight ahead. "It kept me up all night."

Tilly distanced herself from the man. She walked back toward her maid cart as she spoke, "Which were you in again? What number?"

"Eleven," Freddie answered. Of course it was eleven, yes of course. She felt she was going to choke on the air now, suffocate and die on the floor of the lobby.

"Well maybe there's a critter in there, we'll have a look." Tilly continued her work. "Sorry about your stomach though, that's a shame."

Freddie went around the counter, a rolled up bunch of paper in her hand. She pushed her way out of the lobby's front door, leaving Tilly to deal with it all.

The morning was unusually cool for April. But Freddie didn't notice the breeze. Her apple cheeks still simmered and burned.

Eleven.

She walked down into the valley, kicking rocks with her sneakers. A small collection of dusty, green cacti watched her as she made her way to the plateaus. Freddie always thought this bunch of prickly plants looked human, like a lost family in the middle of the desert, hunched together in fright.

The Rainbow was distant now, just a blot on the landscape. She was far enough to take the lighter out, to feel the weight of it in her eager hand. But she would wait until she was obstructed by the small hill to use it.

A vehicle from Fort Bliss rumbled by the motel, a tank looking thing with camo painted on all sides. She had seen it pass by a thousand times, a million.

As Freddie walked, she wondered if Tilly was still being nice to the weird man. Tilly was stronger than her, she was only eighteen, but she was stronger.

Freddie stopped and took in a few breaths. This walk was getting to be too much, too hard on her. She would be seventy soon and she was fat. But those factors didn't change the need for release. In fact, as she aged, she found her troubling diversion to have an even more anchoring pull on her.

She was alone with the scorpions and the vultures. A circle of the ugly birds turned in the air about a mile north. Freddie's ears filled with the rustle of the paper in her hand. She was thankful for the sound, for a different sound. She couldn't think of the scratching.

She was properly obstructed, and had found her little divot, her little pit. She felt instantly at peace once she saw the ash and melted plastic.

She shook as she lit the paper on fire. She held the burning clump in her hands, watching the brilliant colors as she slowly turned her creation. The fire glowed in front of her eyes, making her big, fleshy nose warm with comfort. Regretfully, Freddie dropped the blazing paper into her collection of scorched items before the fire could reach her fingers.

She had restored herself. She could feel the calmness in her mind. She didn't have to think about the acidic smell of vomit anymore, or the way the man stared ahead, or the scratching, scratching, scratching.

Freddie stuck out her hands and surveyed her motionless fingers. She wasn't trembling anymore. She could fool Tilly for a few hours and then find time to come out again, after lunch, with something bigger and juicier to burn. She would treat herself today with a real treasure, a unique find.

~

"What a time for a smoke break!" Tilly exclaimed when Freddie returned to the Rainbow's lobby. "While you were out having your cigarette, I practically had to unhinge Mr. Abbot's fingers from the couch!"

Freddie watched Tilly's exasperated hand waving. She loved her. Not like the girls she loved before, from afar and with a burning passion, but with a motherly love.

"It smelled like shit in here," Freddie shrugged. She plopped down in her usual chair behind the counter, the reality of her age and weight starkly clear as she tried to make herself comfortable. She flipped open one of her ledgers, ready to stare at numbers for the morning. They would be bad, in the red, but that didn't matter anymore. Not really.

Tilly poured herself a coffee and filled it with two packets of Splenda and a hazelnut creamer. "I think we better not let out room eleven until we get some dude to come in and check it out for a pest."

Freddie nodded.

"You know to be honest," Tilly took a sip. "I thought I heard scratching in there the other day, but I just, I don't know I thought I was imagining it."

Freddie shuddered. The tremble returned to her hands in less than a second. "You heard it too?"

"Yeah, you did then?"

"Oh, uh, maybe a bit." Freddie lied. She would never forget the first time she heard it. It had been about four days previously, a rather slow day for the Rainbow Inn. Tilly had been making little comments that day, suggesting she might leave soon, that her life would be changing and she was "growing up."

These words had shaken Freddie to the core. She was going to lose the one person in her life. She could feel the tenuous string between them; taut and ready to snap. Freddie was checking each room for a forgotten item, something under the bed or behind the bathroom door she could bring out to her burning place. Her mind was fixed on a brush or a comb, something with tufts of hair to scorch off. Freddie left room ten unsatisfied. She made her way down the elongated wooden porch to eleven. As she got ready to stick the key in the lock, a sound came from the inside of the door. She stepped back immediately, nearly losing her balance and falling a few inches off the porch into the gravel lot. Instead, she steadied herself on her old, wobbly legs and listened.

It had been a long, deliberate scratch by a single sharp nail, or claw, or knife. Then it came once more, a slow dragging against the door marked eleven. Freddie was sure her mouth hung open and her small, beady eyes felt as though they would pop from her head like marbles.

The room is empty. There's no one there.

An unexpected bubble soared up Freddie's stomach and into her throat. She felt queasy as though the air around room eleven was tainted.

She watched Tilly through the glass wall of the lobby, texting her boyfriend with one hand and eating a small bag of Cheetos with the other.

"He….Hello? Maid, here." Freddie dared to tap on the door. She stepped backward carefully this time, the ring of keys swinging in her hand. "Is there som…."

Now came a flurry of scratches, loud and at once. Freddie stuffed fingers in her mouth to stop from screaming. It sounded like a rabid dog, a trapped raccoon, but no, she knew it was something worse, someone had arrived to punish her. She ran straight into the gravel and then around the side of the Rainbow. She ran, breasts flopping like mad, until she was in her burning place. With no other option she grabbed a handful of prickly sage brush and set it on fire.

~

"God, I wonder what it is. A big rat you think?" Tilly's voice stirred Freddie out of her remembrance. "I don't think I want to go and clean in there today. That guy looked like he'd seen a, oh I don't know, something bad."

Freddie could only nod along weakly. If others could hear the scratches, if the man could and dear Tilly too, then maybe it was an animal after all. Maybe she just scared herself over nothing. Even women of her age could still come up with fantastical stories she supposed.

Tilly pushed her cart full of cleaners and soaps out the lobby door. She was mumbling about some other possible vermin that could crawl into the window of room eleven and make a home. Freddie didn't really hear her. She could think only of the first scratch, slow and controlled. It kept ringing in her ears like a peculiar alarm with no off switch. She would do anything to make the awful sound leave her memory.

Freddie spent the rest of the morning trying to catalogue different things to burn. Things in all her decades of life she still hadn't burned. But as she sat at the Rainbow Inn's counter, watching the few customers leave in their vans and filthy pick-ups, she was persistently reminded of room eleven. She couldn't quite see it from where she sat, but she could see Tilly's cart parked outside of it. She could call someone, an exterminator, and he could come and spray the room or some such nonsense. But Freddie knew, she knew. She could burn all the napkins and plastic dolls in the world, but it wouldn't stop her knowing.

She had tried to scorch the wrong thing, nearly thirty years ago, and now, for some reason, she would have to listen to that insufferable scratching, and even she guessed if she burned down the Rainbow itself, and oh, how she had dreamt of it, she would still hear that long, measured scrape in her ugly ears.

Freddie rose from her seat, determined to pull Tilly out of eleven, to wrap hazard tape around the door and never let anyone enter it again. It wouldn't stop the sound, but it could stop that look, that strange faraway look the man had before he vomited. Freddie pounded down the wooden walkway with purpose.

"Tilly! Tilly get out of there!"

The door was open and it was dark inside. A pile of fresh towels lay on the green carpet. Freddie stepped over them. An icy realization filled her mind.

"Tilly?" She snapped on the lights.

Tilly lay on the bed. She was on her stomach; her blonde hair covering her eyes. All Freddie could think of was U.T.E.P in black, official lettering -- Ms. Matilda Forrest.

Freddie brushed the hair back from Tilly's face. It was perhaps the first time she had actually touched her. Tilly stared into death with youthful eyes. There was a red mark on her neck, a hint of a handprint.

Something rumbled within Freddie. A rage she had never
known, never allowed herself to feel. Even through all the
rejection, the disgust of the women she loved, the dismissal
of her existence by others simply because of her disagreeable
face, she had never felt this anger before.

"You fucking bitch," Freddie whispered to the room.
Each world trembled as it left her mouth. "YOU FUCKING
CUNT!"

She knew why now, why such a random number of years
between what she did and the revenge now coming down
upon her. It was because she finally loved someone, she
finally saw the good in another person and the bitch wanted
to take it from her. For once she loved something more than
she loved fire.

For the second time in four days Freddie ran, but this
time she had a purpose greater than scorched sage brush. She
flung the door open of the shed behind the motel and quickly
located a shovel and a large canvas tarp. She swung the tarp
over her shoulder and dragged the heavy tool behind her.

She moved past her burning place, her own chest feeling
as though it were filled with sizzling coals of rage. She began
to slow, marching on into the desert, the afternoon sun
raging hot in the sky above her. She passed a familiar crop of
desert sunflowers and made a turn toward a ridge of rock.
She was sweating from the heat and the anger. She wondered
if the circle of vultures would soon come to find her, if they
could smell her aged body on the brink of disaster.

She found the cluster of red rocks she was searching for
and kneeled beside them. She breathed in the dusty air and
began to talk to the woman under the ground.

"Tilly, Tilly, why?" Freddie was surprised by her own
tears. "Why did you have to take her? I didn't even do it, I
didn't even burn the damn thing."

There was no answer.

Freddie stood, not bothering to brush off the desert sand
from her khaki slacks. Instead she began to dig with large
dramatic strokes. The shovel rubbed her hands raw, but she
did not stop. She dumped each load of earth into a pile,

waiting for the sound. The sound of metal on bone. Then it came, like a miracle, somehow louder and more distinct than the constant scratch in her ears. This made her dig faster, reveling in the feel of the hard vibration as her shovel hit the woman under the ground. Freddie finally peered down into the hole she had created and was pleased with the sight.

The skull was right where she had left it, twenty eight years previously, along with all the other white bones, big and small, that make up a human. Freddie got on her knees and fished each part out; the hole was only about two feet deep.

Why had she stopped the fire all those years ago? Why hadn't she burned the skeleton too, along with the clothes and flesh she watched melt off like wax? That was why the woman had come back, that was why she took Tilly.

Freddie placed the collected bones in the tarp and dropped them in the hole once again. She lit the edge of the canvas with her lighter, the satisfaction enveloping her entire body. The bones of the wretched bitch from room eleven roasted in the blaze. Freddie would sit and wait until there was nothing but a flickering flame and white powder.

The same military vehicle, or perhaps one just like it, rumbled down the highway. She was farther out, but she could still see it. It made Freddie realize she was stuck on an endless loop of days, this one no different than the day the woman in room eleven left her dog to bark like crazy.

~

It was 1987 and Freddie was thirty-six years old. Her father had just died, leaving her to tend to the Rainbow all alone. So she prowled the rooms when the customers were out driving around looking for cheap fast food.

That night Freddie was desperate to find something. She discovered that the lady in room eleven liked girls too, Freddie could tell by the way she wore her hair, and, also, by a rather intimate Polaroid tucked into the lining of her suitcase. And she had a real yappy dog, an ankle biter, that nibbled at Freddie's feet with tiny, yet razor sharp teeth.

Freddie knew the type of dog was a Pomeranian, because of its tell-tale ginger fur and cottony tail. As she slipped the tantalizing picture back into its hiding spot, she thought for the first time about taking the dog to the burning place. She had never done a dog before, only mice and scorpions and once an already dead cat.

She picked up the little ball of fluff; it weighed hardly anything at all, and quietly backed out of room eleven. She made sure no other customers were milling about and then carried the tiny dog out back. She held its shaking muzzle with one hand to stop it from barking. She didn't know she was being followed as she snaked through the cacti and tumbleweeds to get to her burning place. A part of her mind urged her to stop. It was a dog, a living thing. Yet the thought of watching the flames lick its pink little face made her tense with excitement. Her mind wanted her to think of the after, of the hysterical woman looking for her dog. But she pushed this aside and dropped the animal in her makeshift pit. It began to yelp and scratch at the dirt sides. Freddie was considering how best to proceed when she heard the crackle of dead brush under a stranger's foot.

The dog's owner stood with a hand on each hip and a flash of disbelief in her eyes. She was older than Freddie, by a few decades, but in much better physical shape. Her deeply tanned muscular arms indicated an active person, one used to hiking in the Texas mountains. She swiftly walked over to the burning place and removed her pet from the pile of debris.

"I don't know what you think you're doing," the woman began. "But I intend to call the police." She huffed. The dog, now calm in her mother's arms, seemed to nod along in agreement with the woman's threat.

Freddie dropped the gold lighter in her hand, the same one she kept in her pocket nearly thirty year later, and lunged at the women from room eleven. The dog yelped in surprise as it was flung to the ground. The woman toppled over as Freddie jumped onto her and pushed her into the dirt.

"Run, Delilah! Run!"

The little dog actually obeyed, looking over its furry shoulder one last time before bolting into the endless desert.

Freddie strangled the woman in the dark. She pushed down on her throat so easily, so naturally. In fact she stayed that way, holding the woman's neck, long after she stopped breathing. The woman, although strong and desperate to live, couldn't fight against Freddie's anger, her embarrassment. No one had seen the burning place.

~

Now she sat watching the woman burn for the second time because apparently the first time hadn't done the trick. Somehow the dead hag had managed to kill her Tilly.

Freddie leaned back on her old, creaking arms, taking in a deep inhale of smoke. It pleased her to do this now, to send the last remnants of the woman from room eleven to Hell with the purging power of fire.

She couldn't even hear the scratching over the sound of the bones popping and fizzling in the blaze.

"Yip!"

Freddie looked up from her task. She could see an edge of the Rainbow, mirage like in the fiery El Paso sun. There was an animal beside the building, small and dancing on impossibly tiny feet.

"Yip! Yip," it barked.

"No." Freddie shook her head. "No….it couldn't…" Although she was in her sixties Freddie had never needed glasses. Good eyesight was her one super power, a single favor from her mistake of a body. So she could see the dog perfectly well. The same one that ran off alone into the desert on a fall night twenty eight years ago.

Delilah raised a single paw and dropped it in the dirt. She twirled in a circle, excited and anxious for Freddie to follow her.

"Oh! Oh!" Freddie carefully got in a kneeling position and then stood. Her pinched face was now purple with rage and effort. "YOU! YOU KILLED TILLY!" She screamed.

Delilah wiggled her puff of a tail and leapt up onto the wooden porch connecting the rooms of the Rainbow. She disappeared around the corner.

Freddie left the burning place. She couldn't run anymore. She could only walk in stilted steps, punctuated by the beat of her rasping breath.

"That dog, that DOG!" She spat through her tight mouth. She should have charred it all those years ago; she should have gone after it and pulled it back to the burning place. It could have simmered on top of its mother. Yipping and clawing until it burned up. Then Tilly would still be alive.

Freddie stepped into room eleven, not bothering to avoid the fresh towels still strewn in the door way. A wisp of air conditioning coming from the unit underneath the window made her suddenly aware of how much sweat snaked down her rotund body. Her swinging breasts tacked together like sticky buns.

"Where are you? Oh little doggy? Where are you girl?" She closed the door behind her and crept inside. Tilly still lay on the double bed, one hand limply hanging, so that her knuckles grazed the moldy carpet.

It occurred to Freddie that she should have brought the shovel along to brain the dog. But as she stood in room eleven she couldn't help but remember that Delilah, as her owner called her, was surely already dead. She had probably been chewed up by coyotes in the 80s. But this realization meant nothing, because she heard a familiar whiny bark coming from under the bed.

Freddie felt for the bulge in her pocket. It was there, ready to burn. She sank down on her stomach and peered under the bottom of the comforter and into the blackness. Aside from a stale smell there was nothing. No tag jangled on a collar. There was no hot dog breath in her face. She swiped her arms about in hopes of feeling fur, but there was no dog.

As she resigned to give up, Freddie felt a ripping pain in her ankle. For a split second she thought it was age itself, reminding her with joint aches to slow down. But her hand instinctively went toward the sting and she could feel a fuzzy head. Delilah's sharp teeth were embedded in her ankle. Hot blood poured into her white sock and atop her sneaker. Freddie kicked the dog off, screaming in pain.

"Oh you little....you little bitch!" Freddie was still on her stomach and she began to crawl toward the yipping dog. Delilah had a bit of blood on her well-trimmed face. Her black eyes watched Freddie with mirth. She was enjoying this. She wanted this.

Freddie, now up on her hands and knees, moved closer to the dog in the corner. She felt for the lighter and produced it, showing it to Delilah.

"See this," the gold glinted in the sunlight streaming in through the window. "I'm going to light you on fire." Freddie absently pulled at her bloody sock. "I should've done it a long time ago, you were always supposed to burn."

Delilah let out a high pitched bark as though to answer. Then she skittered along the wall and jumped up into an armchair. Freddie crawled behind with one hand while she flicked the lighter with the other. The dog didn't seem to notice the pursuing woman. Instead, she stopped to nibble an itch on her back leg.

Freddie stopped, her face inches from the dog, and applied her lighter to the chair. The fabric covered arm began to blaze. She couldn't help but watch the dance of the flames, the intoxicating mix of orange and yellow.

Delilah watched the flames too. But her furry face wore an expression of boredom. Smoke swirled into her nostrils, but she did not bark or cough or move. An errant spark lit the curtains on fire.

Freddie sat on the floor, taking in her handy work. She looked to see if the dog was bothered or scared yet. It was gone. The blazing chair was empty.

"What?" She spun her head around searching for the tiny dog that killed Tilly. The room was filling with smoke rather rapidly.

A slow, deliberate scratching sound filled the room.

Freddie shuddered. She covered both ears with her hands and howled, "I'LL KILL YOU! I'M GONNA BURN YOU!"

More scratching. Louder. Claws on a door. Nails on a chalkboard. Coming from inside her. The sound was IN her ears, she couldn't escape it. Freddie began to light everything on fire, the comforter underneath Tilly, the carpet, and the folder with the hotel guide inside.

But the sound of the raging fire could not overwhelm the incessant scratching. As she laid down to die, choking on the blinding smoke, Freddie heard one more sound.

It was Tilly.

"Freddie? FREDDIE? I'm on fire Freddie! FRED! My hair's on FIRE!" The eighteen year old kicked a top the bed, her screams eventually turning into whimpers.

Freddie tried to pull herself up. She wanted to save Tilly, but there was so much smoke. Freddie's lungs hung like lead in her chest.

So that was the trick. The little dog wanted Freddie to be responsible for Tilly's death. She wasn't dead. She was alive.

Until now.

Until Freddie's fire melted her pretty face off.

Fire licked at Freddie's feet. She would finally feel it, feel what it was like to burn.

Through the fog of the smoke, somehow, she saw Delilah outside the window. She was so small, too small. She had to be hovering there, floating. The little animal watched Freddie's pant legs start on fire. She then began to scratch the window. Scratch with her sharp front paws as she smiled, yes, the dog's mouth stretched into a joyful smile as she scratched.

Willoughby

Inside Willoughby Grocery you will find everything you might need for a quick stop. You can purchase three flavors of spaghetti sauce and mint ice cream with little chocolate cows mixed in. You'll find batteries and whipped cream in a can, and you can even pick up Sudoku books and gum at the checkout. But everyone in Willoughby, Minnesota, knows not to shop here for more than a bag full.

Instead they get the kids strapped into the car, iPads in hand, and drive the thirty-five minutes to the Fergus Falls Super Foods. Willoughby Grocery is simply for the times you forgot the olives or the bread, or you couldn't wait another minute for a candy bar.

Amanda knew that her family's store was an in-between; an overpriced convenience, a stop for either the forgetful or the lazy. She quite liked it this way, because it meant her nights at work were spent reading and dreaming.

On this night Amanda had a yellowed paperback, Stephen King's *It*, waiting on the counter while she dusted the cookie packages. Unlike the milk and diapers, the Oreos and vanilla wafers got rather dusty.

"Dylan's grandma is done." Riley Fischer appeared next to her in the aisle.

Amanda tried not to look up at his face. His flirting had recently become more aggressive, and, in even more of a surprise, Amanda had been playing along. She had absolutely no intention of ever dating Riley, but she enjoyed their new banter. That was until he had made a rather awkward pass at her while they were walking home from work.

Since then Amanda had resigned herself to nods and polite small talk. Concentrating on being cold to Riley had been exhausting. It took effort. Amanda felt more natural laughing at his bad jokes and touching his elbow while she told him a story.

"Yup." Amanda stared at the feather duster in her fingers and walked away from Riley. Mrs. Woodhouse stood at the register with a full basket.

"I'm sorry, Mrs. Woodhouse. I hope you weren't waiting long." Amanda gave the old woman a sincere smile.

"No, no. You work so hard, Mandy."

Amanda laughed. "I don't know about that. But you can tell my dad that next time you see him." She began to remove the collection of yogurts from the wire basket.

Each yogurt had an individual orange price sticker. Amanda punched each digit into the register with careful consideration. She wished they had a fancy scan system like Super Foods that gave a satisfying beep for each item. Amanda typed in the codes for two red delicious apples and a bag of sweet corn.

Amanda bagged Mrs. Woodhouse's purchases while the old woman struggled to get her checkbook out of her purse. Riley stood at the front of the store. He waited to walk Mrs. Woodhouse home. It was the aspect of his job he seemed to actually like the most. He carried plastic bags for the elderly citizens of Willoughby. Riley told her how he enjoyed getting outside, breathing in the fresh air, and sometimes he even got tips.

"That's eleven dollars and forty-two cents."

"A pen, dear?"

Amanda handed Mrs. Woodhouse a pen, noticing the yellow, crocheted checkbook cover she had seen hundreds of times before. Amanda was instantly bothered by the familiar object that Mrs. Woodhouse held in her creased hands. It was the wrong time. She had never seen that hideous strip of material at night.

"It's so late. You're never here this late." Amanda motioned toward the large window that looked out on downtown Willoughby. It was deep, black night and there were only a few minutes left until close. The street was already dead. This was a farmer's town, after all.

"Oh yes, just wanted to make a run. I knew Riley would be here to walk me home." The old woman didn't look up from her checkbook. She wrote the date with a shaky hand. "It's a good thing, too."

Amanda nodded. It was still so odd, Mrs. Woodhouse, early riser, here at nearly ten at night. Amanda felt a surprising anxiety building in her belly. Something wrong was going to happen. Not exactly bad, but wrong. Her own grandmother, the one still alive, was surely fast asleep now. She hadn't known an old woman, certainly not one as old and withered as Mrs. Woodhouse, to go out past dinner time. It was unfair, Amanda supposed, to assume anything. Maybe, after a quick stop to drop off her yogurt, Mrs. Woodhouse would be on her way to a Minneapolis dance club. She smiled at the thought. It made her feel better.

"It's a very good thing." The old woman repeated. She stopped writing in order to fish a tissue out of her cardigan pocket. She pressed it to her wrinkled nose and gave a rather impressive blow.

Amanda looked automatically to Riley, widening her eyes to show her annoyance. He gave a toothy smile, his way of agreeing. She took notice of the flush in his cheeks and felt a sudden twinge of regret. She shouldn't have looked his way. He was already reading into her glance, hoping it meant she was ready to flirt and joke again. God, how was she going to be both nice and cold? It would all hopefully become easier next year in college.

Mrs. Woodhouse put her used tissue back in her pocket and took up the pen. "That monster is out there tonight."

"Sorry?" Amanda felt as though she had been physically slapped back into the moment.

The old woman sighed. She finished up her signature, which was just a mess of pointy lines and scraggily curves.

"Oh, the monster. He was out by the Hines' place, hiding behind that, you know that… oh that thing Dan Hines put in their front yard, you know the…"

"The bench swing?" Riley grabbed the two plastic bags of food, ready to deliver.

"Monster?" Amanda squeaked.

Doris Woodhouse smiled, revealing two rows of yellowed, ancient teeth. "Bench swing, yes. Dan Hines is such a show-off. He's going to put a koi pond in, too, you know, next summer I think he said."

"Do you mean an animal?" Riley's eyebrows knit together in confusion. Amanda appreciated his hesitant expression. She knew she had gone pale.

"Oh, oh, no, he's not a fox or bear or anything like that." Mrs. Woodhouse giggled as though the very idea was ridiculous. "But you're a big boy, Riley, you'll protect me." She placed her knotted fingers on Riley's thin arm. He flinched at the old woman's touch.

Amanda watched silently as Doris Woodhouse zipped up her enormous satchel bag and then shuffled across the linoleum toward Willoughby Grocery's front glass door. Riley followed with a brown plastic bag in each hand. He turned toward Amanda and shrugged.

"Good night Mrs. Woodhouse. I'm sure Riley will keep you safe." Amanda hoped to laugh casually, as though she was in on the joke, but an odd sound escaped, wooden and fake.

Riley rushed ahead and pushed the door open. Mrs. Woodhouse raised her hand and gave a quivering wave. She shook, not from fright, but from the inevitable damage of time. The bell sounded as the door swung shut behind them. Riley Fischer and Doris Woodhouse were enveloped by night. The fluorescent store lights reflected on the front windows, making it impossible for Amanda to see the two figures heading down Main.

Immediately Amanda sensed a stifling loneliness.

The Coca-Cola clock ticked like thunder above her head. It was six minutes to ten, close enough. Amanda had to mentally force her feet to move from their place on the floor. She ran to the door and twisted the sign to read "closed." Her dad, of course, would have visibly shuddered at the notion of closing early, but Amanda was eighteen now and in charge.

"Monster," she whispered to the empty store. The word held some sort of power she couldn't explain or understand.

Amanda felt a sudden chill from within, a feeling as though she had overlooked something important. It was the same icy ache that overcame her a few weeks ago when she had crawled into bed and suddenly remembered she had left her essay on British Romanticism in the library printer.

But this was worse.

Amanda locked the deadbolt. Riley would just have to knock if he wanted back in. He would be back. His phone and Velcro wallet were tucked under the register. She busied herself with the closing routine.

She stuffed all the money from the register into a small canvas bag and initialed the log. She tidied the single checkout counter and placed the basket Mrs. Woodhouse had used back with the others. Silence followed her from aisle to aisle as she did a last check. There were no muffled voices coming from the City Café next door. They closed at eight-thirty. Amanda was thankful to note, the funeral home that shared the western wall with Willoughby Grocery was characteristically quiet, too. She hoped Riley would knock soon. Mrs. Woodhouse's Victorian was only three blocks north.

Amanda chided herself for being scared, for letting the old woman's words shake her. In less than a year, she would be away from Willoughby, studying literature at the Main U. She would be in a dorm with a stranger. She might need to walk at night on unfamiliar streets. She would have to get tough. Yet, somehow, the familiar roads of Willoughby were more frightening. Somehow, she believed in monsters here.

Her little town, her place, it had shadows. She knew this.

Amanda waited.

The clock thudded in rhythm.

Why was that clock so damn loud? Amanda cupped her hands on either side of her face and pressed her nose to the front window. There were two dim street lamps revealing nothing but an empty street. There was no wind to push a Styrofoam cup down the concrete. There was no drunk hiccupping while he straddled the curb. Main Street was an abandoned film set, a photograph.

Lanky, awkward Riley did not appear. Amanda pressed her eyes closed and wished. She promised herself that, once he arrived, she would hug him and rub her face into his concave chest. Riley could read whatever he wanted to in her touch. She just wanted to be anchored, to be back in the world where she didn't actually believe Doris Woodhouse. She wanted him to make a stupid joke, and, God, maybe even try to kiss her. That would remind her she was just a silly girl in a silly town occupied by nothing scarier than Mr. Dewitt, the aggressively racist ninety-year-old.

The clock read twelve minutes past ten.

He had left her. Riley had continued on home. She was sure of it now. He had a stick of deer jerky between his lips, and he was in his game chair, starting up his X-Box. Ass.

Amanda steeled herself. She would have to walk alone tonight. She couldn't even text him. His phone was still secure inside the store. She grabbed the canvas bag of cash, her own phone, and the house keys from the drawer, pushing them all into her small backpack. She chided herself for not biking to work that afternoon. She'd had the urge to walk instead, so now she had stranded herself with only her feet to carry her.

"Monsters aren't real," Amanda told Willoughby Grocery.

Her body didn't believe her. Her stomach ached, her mouth was dry. She unlocked the door, pushed it open and then used the keys to lock it from the outside in one fluid motion. Amanda walked into nothing. No one was on Main, no car headlights cutting through the gloom, and no couples on a walk enjoying the mild, fall night.

This is Willoughby, her home.

Yet Amanda couldn't shake her fear, couldn't forget the word "monster" as it pounded in her head with the same predictable beat of the Coca-Cola clock. She passed the funeral home, and then the drug store, and then she met with the curb where Main intersected with Ash. She walked onto Ash Street's sidewalk into the darkness.

All the houses were still and black.

Everyone is asleep. Jesus. It's Friday night. Amanda noticed a blue flickering light from the Hines' living room. *Thank you, thank you. At least Dan Hines watches the Late News.*

She stopped.

The Hines' white bench swing rocked as though it were caught in a breeze. Amanda didn't feel anything in the air, but the absence of wind. *The monster, he was hiding behind that, you know that...*

"Oh, oh shit." Amanda's legs were heavy. That familiar chill rattled her heart. That overwhelming notion she had forgotten something vital rushed inside her mind. *You're a big boy, Riley, you'll protect me.*

She pitched forward. Her dense feet, seemingly encased in cement, wouldn't budge. Amanda spun her arms frantically, searching for an impossible rope, or invisible life raft, to save her from the night.

Amanda begged her feet to move. The swing rocked noisily, moved by some alien force in the windless night. She had a sudden memory of Riley, much younger with a smooth, craterless face. She had been alone in the T-ball field, her limbs frozen. She stood in an awkward dance-like pose, her legs about to slide into the splits. She waited for him to unfreeze her. Riley ran up to her side, breathing heavy from the game and considered the best place to rest his small hand. He touched her on the nose with one finger, and she imagined herself, like a magical toy from the Nutcracker, awakening into a new reality. She ran ahead of Riley into the open field. It had been the summer before fifth grade, and it had been undoubtedly their most epic game of freeze tag.

Amanda wished Riley was there now to press her on the nose so she could unfreeze. Instead she focused on the unnatural movement of the Hines' swing. It moved with a jittery, unpredictable clatter that made Amanda think of something animal. Something rustling beneath it.

It wasn't an animal. Amanda knew this as well as she knew that there was no one on the streets of Willoughby to help her. She looked up Ash and saw the outline of Doris Woodhouse's imposing Victorian. Somehow every window was black. Not just black, but each window was a void.

Amanda pitched forward. Finally her feet obeyed and came with the rest of her. She made her way up the sidewalk, keenly aware of the Hines' swing. It had stopped creaking. She supposed the monster was finding a new hiding place, or, perhaps, he followed right behind her. If she turned, he would be at her heels like a lost puppy.

She laughed at the notion of him being in any way puppy-like. She knew what it looked like. Her mind's eye had his figure stored inside. She knew his snout and eyes were wolfish, yet he had no fur. His skin had a human texture, but was starkly white, mottled with brown veins. He could both stand and crawl with ease. Amanda didn't want to think of his mouth. She couldn't picture it. She was oddly relived the image was not accessible.

Reaching the edge of Mrs. Woodhouse's black, wrought-iron fence, Amanda stopped. She considered using the enormous crow-shaped knocker on the front door and knocking until her hands bled. Just to ask a question. Just to see a human. But Amanda knew Mrs. Woodhouse would not answer her door. Amanda could knock until, well, until he wrapped her in his muscular front legs and began to chew. But Mrs. Woodhouse would sit in the darkness. Because that is what they all did. Amanda knew this.

So instead she picked up the pace and walked on wobbly legs a few more blocks north, to the last paved street of Willoughby. Amanda made a left. Although the darkness was overwhelmingly complete, she could make out the lines of her house.

The windows were all black, as she knew they would be, but the sense of closeness was intoxicating to her. Soon, she would hug her mother. Soon, she would be in bed. Soon, she would forget.

Amanda passed her neighbors, determined to make it to her front step. She kept her eyes on the family home, recognizing each corner and line. Unexpectedly, she made out the shape of something else, something not right. It shifted in the darkness, moving with the same stilted uneasiness as the swing.

"Hello?" Amanda swallowed down a sick rise of phlegm. *Oh, oh, no, he's not a fox or bear or anything like that.*

The creature sat on her front porch. He had been waiting for her on the top step. He rose as Amanda stopped at the end of the gravel driveway. She noted how he blinked his yellow eyes in an oddly human manner. She recognized his hairless tail as it wrapped, like a snake, around his torso.

Amanda dropped her backpack. It was now, in this moment, at the end of her drive, that it all came crashing into her. She knew this monster; she knew him as well as she knew all the residents of her tiny town.

He was there; he was always there. He had been born in Willoughby, and, like most of the residents, he would stay there until he died. If he died. Amanda found no comfort in this new realization and instead began to run back up the street into the blackness.

He was behind her of course, and she knew why. It was past ten, and she was alone, and she'd forgotten. She began devising a safe route, but then the thought struck her, was there really a safe way?

Amanda found herself in the Olson's yard. Just like every other house in Willoughby, the Olson's was murky and quiet. She didn't bother screaming. Her throat was full of salty mucus and her lips were pressed together in a line.

The monster's jaws were wide and noisy. He made guttural growls as he ran behind her. He sounded more annoyed than hungry. Amanda pulled herself over the Olson's chain-link gate and fell onto the paver stones that wrapped around the house leading to the backyard. She followed the stones, vague rectangles in the night, much like Dorothy on her yellow brick road.

She followed them like they would lead her to another reality, another town. Instead they brought her to a small shed, inevitably stuffed with rusted tools, and, also, inevitably locked. The wolfish creature gained on her. He wasn't running, but he rather crawled on all fours. She looked over her shoulder and saw his glowing eyes just on the other side of the Olson's backyard. He paced by the gate, watching her, breathing and drooling.

Even on his knees he was enormous. Had he always been so big? Amanda didn't know. She had never been this close to him, close enough to feel his angry heat. When she locked up Willoughby Grocery, Riley had always been there to walk her home. And how had he gotten home?

She had never asked herself this before. He just always had, and she'd always forgotten. She was sure he forgot, too. Everyone in Willoughby did. She knew this now. She knew they all forgot.

Amanda stared back at her stalker. She began to accept her fate. It was past ten, and she roamed Willoughby alone. That was just unacceptable. The thing with claws, he didn't have a name, although Amanda thought at that moment, as she pressed her body against the side of the tool shed, that he should have a name, like all town mascots, knew she had broken the rule. She was fair game.

She actually felt a strangled laugh push through her lips. The creature watched with his jaundiced eyes. He swayed upon his hind legs and then actually sniffed the air, like Amanda's dachshund did before he settled on a spot to squat. Amanda wanted to laugh again but decided against it. She covered her mouth with a shaking hand, conscious of the monster's rage.

He was going to eat her, and it was going to hurt. Amanda had that cold sensation, that one she got when she forgot something. She felt the cold prickly pins on her arms and frozen ice in her belly.

Her book.

She had forgotten *It* on the counter, next to the cough drops and gum. Well, it didn't matter now, did it? At least her book was safe; it wouldn't be chewed and swallowed like she was going to be.

"We're open till ten," Amanda told the monster.

He shifted somehow, back and forth, insect-like. Amanda knew he could shift like that across the grass and kill her in less than a second. He could rip her with his teeth. No, no, they weren't teeth.

Amanda remembered why she had forced the image of his mouth from her mind. His jaws crunched with needles, thousands of them. When he opened his mouth, the sharp barbs would shine in the moonlight. It would be like a smile before he shoved her down his ravenous throat. She knew that now, and she had known that before. But she had always forgotten.

Amanda took a small step backward. And then another. He didn't move forward, but he shifted to the side. She swallowed more salty fear hoping the vomit wouldn't come. If she stopped to spit, that would surely be the vulnerable moment he would take her. She couldn't think of that now.

She wanted to think of Riley unfreezing her limbs, of her dad stocking shelves, of her mom reading Emily Dickinson poetry to her. Her last thoughts might as well be pleasant. Maybe that would make her taste bad. Maybe fear was delicious. Amanda dared another step backward. She was in total darkness. She regarded the moon, an unhelpful sliver. There were no porch lights illuminating her or the creature.

Although she couldn't really see it, she knew there was a shovel. She sensed the presence of it next to her, behind her really. It was propped against the shed. Mr. Olson had used it to dispatch a pesky groundhog that evening. She knew that, too. Her hands found the wooden handle. It was smooth.

Amanda picked up the shovel and swung it in front of her with all the bravery she could muster. She thrust the implement up behind her shoulder, bringing it down to hit the ground again; the monster shifted. This time, he shifted right in front of her, inches, and she hit with full force.

The air pushed out of his jaw of needles, and he fell to his abdomen in the grass. Amanda raised the shovel, and came down again. She couldn't untangle her sounds from his. They both panted, and squeaked, and growled.

Amanda hit him again and again.

She felt warm fluid on her face and arms. He lay beneath her, hurt but not dead. She could see only night. The wolfish thing gurgled below her, a pile of shadow, a lump of dirty clothes, an amorphous nothing.

She dropped the shovel and ran from the Olsons' yard, leaping the gate in one clumsy jump. She ran to her driveway, covered in warmth but still cold in her stomach. She had to remember. She had to remember she could hurt him. He bled, he couldn't die, but he could be stopped. Temporarily immobilized. She could hurt him, and win, and go home. She had to remember to ask Riley if this is what he did each night, if he used a shovel or a gun or a hammer or an axe.

She had to ask Doris Woodhouse what she knew about the monster. If she remembered; she had to remember.

Amanda's leg burned. She had hit her own shin with the shovel, and her blood spilled onto her sneaker. Maybe that would help. The stitches and the pain, maybe they would help her remember. She just had to remember.

Amanda's dachshund, Toby, greeted her at the door. He twisted his long body in excitement and worry. Dim light shone from her parent's bedroom. Amanda pulled herself over the threshold and fell into the front hall. Toby licked her injured leg, trying his best to clean her up. She kissed his head, thankful for his kindness. She was safe. She felt it instantly. She got up and hobbled to the light at the end of the carpeted hall.

"Hey, Mom." Amanda poked her head into the bedroom. "I'm home."

Amanda's mother looked up from her book. Her husband slept beside her. "Did Riley walk you home? It's so late." She couldn't see blood.

Amanda nodded. "Yeah mom, he always does." She didn't lie. Amanda knew Riley must have walked beside her, his signature bottle of pop in hand. She looked down at her wound. It was just a scratch. She would look for a bandage in the bathroom.

"What's wrong?" Amanda's mom raised her head from the pile of pillows and watched her daughter. Amanda looked pale.

"Nothing. I just, I just forgot something." Amanda sensed the familiar ice in her veins.

"Hmm, what?"

It came to Amanda then, what she had forgotten. "Damn, my book. I was going to finish it."

ABOUT THE AUTHOR

Meg Hafdahl was raised in British Columbia, Canada, and Duluth, Minnesota. She studied literature and creative writing at the University of Minnesota-Duluth, where she received a grant for playwriting. Her short story Dark Things was a recent finalist for the 2014 Jane Austen Short Story Award.

She has published short stories with Spider Road Press in their anthology *Eve's Requiem*, as well as with Inklings Publishing in the *Eclectically Criminal* anthology.

Currently, Meg lives in Rochester, Minnesota, with her husband and two young sons.